.

UNA CITA EN SANTIAGO

Luis Garcia in Chile

Gail Chiarello

Workwomans Press
Seattle

Poems and songs:
"The Playground," "A Morning in Santiago,"
"The Calculated Lion,"
from The Calculated Lion Copyright © Luis Garcia 1963
UNA CITA EN SANTIAGO
"Piano Solo," "The Vices of the Modern World," "Montaña
Rusa," "Jovenes," "El Tunel," "La Vibora,"
From Anti-Poems Copyright © Nicanor Parra 1960
Translated by Jorge Elliott
City Lights Books The Pocket Poets Series 1960
and/or from
Poems and Antipoems Copyright © Nicanor Parra
With translations by Miller Williams
New Directions 1967

"Canción del Minero," "No Canto Por Cantar,"
From Antologia Musical Victor Jara

ISBN 978-0-9820073-5-8
First Printing March 2014

Workwomans Press
Seattle
www.workwomanspress.com

UNA CITA EN SANTIAGO

Luis Garcia May 1967

for Luis

on the occasion of his 75th birthday

Contents

Chapter One

His twenty-fourth birthday party had also been Luis's farewell to Berkeley. The leave-taking had been marked by the usual last-minute disorder. His new passport had gone missing until Wefe found it tucked into Robert Creeley's *For Love* as a place mark. His mother insisted on putting a wool sweater in his over-stuffed valise, although it would be summer in Chile. His father gave him a stack of traveler's checks with the stern advice not to cash them all at once.

The next day he was on his way to Chile with Wefe. The trip from SFO took seventy-two hours. He and Wefe had barely slept. The plane refueled in Ecuador, at a desolate tropical landing strip. A corrugated-metal Quonset hut served as the passenger terminal and its single Coca-Cola machine glowed red-and-white at the edge of the green jungle. No one was allowed off the plane. Finally Wefe fell asleep on his shoulder. She smelled of Breck shampoo and lily of the valley, his lovely, delicate Wefe. So tender, so innocent, so in need of his guidance. But Luis was unable to relax. He was charged with anticipation, with adrenaline.

Across the aisle, a woman with long Rita Hayworth tresses, wearing a pink sheath and jacket, smiled at him. She had a broad face. "First trip to Santiago?" she asked in a Spanish-accented English. There was something forward in her manner which excited him. Wefe's shoulder was leaning into his; Luis heard her slight, delicate snore.

"Ah, Santiago. A nice city. But you must visit Valparaiso. It is my city. It means Valley of Paradise. It is on the sea and so very beautiful." Her eyes seemed to take him in, up and down, the length of him. Were all South American women as sexy and forward as she was? Wefe stirred against his shoulder but did not wake up.

"The flamenco dancer, Antonio Gades? You look like him. You are Spanish, no?"

"Spanish by descent," Luis said. "A poet, not a dancer." He launched into his story, feeling her attentive eyes on him.

Fred Langhorst had invited Luis to join him and his daughter for Fred's Fulbright year in Santiago. Fred was a well-known Berkeley architect. A year with him and his daughter and their circle would have untold intellectual benefits. His parents had been skeptical. But Luis was used to cajoling. The parents relented. There could be an educational allowance. In fact, he was going to Chile on scholarship, so to speak, an award from his grandfather's Mertins Foundation. But Luis would have to continue his studies. He would enroll at the Universidad Católica.

"The father invited you?" said the dark-haired woman. "Then there's marriage in your future?"

"No marriage in my future," said Luis. It was true when Fred made his invitation, Luis wondered if he were being invited as the future son-in-law. He and Wefe had had a serious conversation. It was too soon to think of marriage. They loved each other, but each would be free. Wefe said they would be like Jean-Paul Sartre and Simone de Beauvoir. Luis agreed. He liked de Beauvoir's remark, "I had no intention of interfering with Sartre's need to sample the infinite variety of women who would come his way." That sounded good to Luis, although possibly unlikely.

"We Chileans love our poets," said the dark-haired woman. She reached in her purse and handed him a little scented card. "If you are ever in Valparaiso, give me a call." Luis thrust it into his pocket, trying not to awaken Wefe.

An hour out from Santiago, Luis had dozed off when Wefe shook him awake. There was a commotion. Passengers

2

were standing in the aisle, crowding to peer out of the windows on the left. Luis feared that the collective weight of all their bodies would cause the 707 to lose balance. He followed their gaze. Smoke was billowing from the propellers. One of the plane's engines was failing. The premonition of imminent disaster had become a certainty. His heart flew up into his mouth.

Now the turbo-prop Boeing 707 was skimming so close over the cordillera that Luis García feared it would crash into the peaks. The saw teeth of the Andes were silhouetted, strange knobs with brutal angles and black hatchet shapes, against a sky streaked peach, rose, blood orange. These mountains looked hungrier than California's Sierras, more ruthless than the Rockies. They resembled blank, expressionless faces, almost certainly hostile, of a group of pre-Inca shamans.

This was it. The end, before it had even begun.

The 707 lurched and dipped, then its wheels touched the tarmac. After a few hundred yards the plane came to a stop. A flotilla of six fire trucks, *bomberos*, was rolling toward them. They had arrived at the Aeropuerto de Punahuel.

That was his entrée to Santiago. It was January 1963.

At the beginning of March Luis matriculated in the Universidad Católica. The campus on the Alameda was beautiful. A quadrangle of bright green grass and small trees was surrounded by shadowy arcades with stone arches, where *los hermanos* walked, their black robes fluttering behind them.

But when the Jesuit brothers gave the assignment for the first week—go home and read one hundred pages of Calderón's *La Vida Es Sueño,* Luis was uneasy. Chilean Spanish sounded nothing like the *español* he had studied in Berkeley. Words were all run together; s's were barely

3

pronounced; y's and double ll's were munch-mouthed. He could not follow the lectures. Many days it required all of his powers simply to respond to the morning roll call.

"*¿Don Luis García?*"

"*Presente.*"

The students at U-Católica came from Chile's upper class. They had English surnames and Spanish ones— Mackenna or Peters or Edwards, as well as Bulnes and Videla and Errázuriz. Most had attended the English boarding school for adolescent boys called St. George's College. They dined with their fathers at the Union Club. They had their own cars and apartments. They spent summers in Italy and London. Yet despite their love affair with all things English, almost none spoke to him, the *gringo*, the *americano*. Luis had only one friend, Osvaldo Güareí, a scholarship student studying to become a teacher. Osvaldo's large, soft face shone with sincerity. He had full cheeks; his thick hair was parted in the middle; he wore a torn grey jacket with stains at the wrists. Like Luis, Osvaldo was invisible to the young scions of U-Católica.

Luis had observed two of the scions around the quadrangle. They had seemed especially arrogant. Santiago Del Campo and Hector Körner Bulnes. Although they had ignored him, it turned out they did not ignore all *americanos*. When they found lovely Wefe Langhorst sitting alone in a café on the Alameda, her long blonde hair streaming over her black jacket, they asked to sit down at her table They apologized but the room was so crowded. Actually Santiago Del Campo had done all the talking. His friend appeared to be the silent type.

Later Wefe introduced her new friends to Luis. She reported that the Del Campo family of Chile was old. Rich. Important. Santiago was in law school to please his father, law school being an entrée to a future filled with tennis, foreign travel, important posts in government. Santiago was athletic, talkative, confident, good-looking. Despite the trust funds and estates, he spoke with feeling about the important role that students played in the social reform of Chile. When he ran for president of the Federación Estudiante de Chile—he called it FeCH—he had given a fiery speech. Students were the future of a new Chile. He easily defeated the Socialist student who had run against him. Santiago Del Campo's picture had landed on page five of *El Mercurio*, the passionate student leader handsome in his suit, white shirt, and tightly knotted tie. Now the president of FeCH was tutoring Wefe on the alliances, dynamics and personalities of Chile's multi-party political system. There was Allende's *Frente Popular*. The *Partida Cristiana Democrática*, the *Partida Radical*. While speaking of these matters, he often deployed an expression, pulling his eyebrows up toward the center of his forehead while the corners drooped. It conveyed mischief and baffled bemusement, as if many things in this world could not be taken seriously. Santiago's English was very good.

"What kind of name is Santiago?" Luis asked Wefe. "His parents named him after the capital of Chile?"

Wefe laughed. "No, dummy, Santiago is the name of his godfather. Santiago Bulnes—Hector's father. The two families are very close."

Wefe reported the Körner Bulneses were even older and richer than the Del Campos. A forebear had been President of Chile. Uncles and great-uncles were ambassadors and senators. There was a huge mine up north. But Hector Körner Bulnes, Santiago's roommate, rarely had much to say. He had a bony face, a long jaw, pale eyes, eyelids without eyelashes. He was studying geology and mining engineering. Overall he was as colorless and unresponsive as the rocks he studied.

Luis García was a heart-throb. He had not seen himself this way, but Wefe said that had been the opinion of all the girls in Berkeley, and from among all these girls, Luis had chosen her. Beautiful Wefe, she of the swan neck and fine bone structure. Sophisticated Wefe, raised in Europe, fluent in Spanish, Italian, French. Talented Wefe who played the harpsichord and painted magical watercolors. Together they listened to Charlie Mingus and Dexter Gordon, and Luis had read her poems by Robert Creeley and William Carlos Williams and García Lorca. They viewed Buñuel's *Un Chien Andalou* at the Cinema Guild on Telegraph. Despite her worldly education on the continent of Europe, Wefe looked up to Luis. She had been happy to be chosen. He was her first serious boyfriend. They had been inseparable for a year.

But now, in Santiago, something was on her mind. Something—or someone—was distracting her.

Friday night Del Campo and Körner Bulnes had hosted a small gathering. Luis, Wefe, and Osvaldo took the elevator to the third floor of a Belle Epôque building on Villavicencio, Luis carrying a few LPs under his arm. Santiago opened the door. He was wearing a tight white polo through which the muscles of his chest and shoulders were clearly visible. The living room opened to a balcony through French doors. A white leather sofa and two arm chairs were arranged around a glass coffee table on which was placed a Waterford vase filled with roses. A Marantz stereo system and a stack of LPs sat on a teak credenza. For a student pad, it was opulent.

A plump girl with amber skin and enormous black eyes had already arrived. She appeared to be about eighteen. Santiago introduced his cousin, Odalís Luco Errázuriz.

"Are you a student at U-Católica also?" Luis asked.

No, she was not at university. Luis noted something sultry and uncertain in the tremble of her mouth. She had completed her studies with the nuns at Maria Villa Academy. For now she was a companion to her godmother. Odalís accompanied the old woman on shopping trips to Paris and London. When they were in Santiago, they devoted themselves to charity. But Odalís would not serve as a companion to the godmother forever.

"Then what?" asked Luis.

"Then I will get married," she said, demurely.

"Here's something for *mis amigos americanos*," Del Campo announced. He stood with his back to them while he put an LP on the Marantz. Soon Ella Fitzgerald's smoky contralto emanated from the speakers, with Count Basie backing her up.

Do I want you?
Oh, my! Do I!

Wefe snapped her fingers, like a hip beatnik chick in Jack Kerouac's *Subterraneans*. Del Campo moved closer to her. Luis tried to ignore them, busying himself with the collection of LPs. Eddie Fisher. *My Fair Lady*. Frank Sinatra. Del Campo's taste ran to mainstream pop. Out of the corner of his eye, he saw Santiago stretch his torso upward. He gave a long yawn, showing off solid pectorals beneath his tight polo. Then he breathed out and stuck his thumbs loosely into his belt.

"Fred is designing our house in Viña Del Mar." He gazed down at Wefe.

Luis looked up at them. Wefe hadn't mentioned this.

"And Hector's father will build it!" Santiago added.

"Build? I thought Hector's family were all senators and ambassadors." Luis sounded churlish, but there it was. It just came out.

"You haven't seen the Körner Bulnes S.A. signs all over Santiago? Körner Bulnes has a block of new apartment buildings going up right now in Barrio Brasil. They had to demolish the old hospital prison. That was a real blast, wasn't it, Hector?" Hector, sitting across from Osvaldo on the leather couch, smiled slightly.

Wefe flicked her hair over her shoulder. "Wow—Dad's designing a house for you. That's so cool." She was twisting and untwisting a solitary strand of long, blonde hair. "I hear Viña del Mar is really pretty. I've never been there."

"I'll have to take you," said Santiago. Then he murmured something in Spanish. Wefe laughed deliciously. She was fluent.

Luis was not so fluent. "Oh, one beeg happy family?" He spoke up with an exaggerated, fakey Spanish accent. He felt like being insulting. "Anyway, man. This Ella Fitzgerald sucks. How about some Charlie Mingus?"

Wefe made a face. "I like Ella."

"Wefe prefers Ella, and I do, too," said Mr. Suave.

Do I want you?
Oh, my! Do I!

He crooned along with Ella while looking down at Wefe. Now he closed his eyes and rolled his head from side to side. The cool cat. It was pathetic. Luis tried to catch Wefe's eye so they could exchange a knowing glance which would signify, *Del Campo is a jerk.* But Wefe's face was turned up toward Del Campo's.

Do I want you?
Oh, my! Do I!

It was fairly horrible. The LP spun on,

Like Jack Horner,
In the corner,

with Santiago crooning, "Your keeses are worth waiting for!" Luis had a strong desire to grab Del Campo by the throat.

Odalís was jiggling her foot as she looked through a magazine. Luis noticed Osvaldo glancing at her surreptitiously. It was clear he didn't have the confidence to talk to her, thought Luis. He moved the needle, cutting Ella off. "Sorry, man, I can't take these crooners." He held up a Charlie Mingus LP. "Okay?"

The finger-snapping stopped. Del Campo's eyes narrowed for a second; then he rearranged his face. "Súper," he said, smoothly. Suddenly he became the solicitous host. "Hey, I almost forgot! The drinks!" He clapped his hands. "Pisco sour? Jack Daniels? Fernet-and-Coke?"

"Jack Daniels," said Luis.

"White wine," said Wefe.

The stark notes of Hampton Hawes's piano filled the room, above Mingus's bass line. The tune was Yesterdays. Each note filled its space perfectly. This was much better. Luis took a deep breath. He moved over to Wefe. "So Fred's designing a house for the Del Campos?"

"Dad mentioned something in Viña del Mar."

"We should go out there. Check out the beach." His tone was so falsely hearty.

"Yeah, I guess so."

Santiago set a tray of drinks on the coffee table. Luis grabbed a thick square glass of whiskey and took a gulp. The desire to strangle Del Campo was making his fingers tingle. Now Santiago returned to the record player. He lifted the needle up in midbeat and put on a new record. The unctuous trills of Nat King Cole filled the room. Luis groaned. He gave up. He would have to drop the battle of the turntable. He glanced around. Hector was pointing a finger at Osvaldo. Luis had missed something.

"You Bolsheviks are trying to destroy Chile." Hector's bony face had some pink in it. "Fomenting strikes all over the country with your goddamn Marxist pamphlets. All printed by the same little presses. Like those Arancibia Brothers out in Independencia. Someone should close them down."

Luis was counting on a little press to print a book of his some day—maybe Graham Mackintosh's press in San Francisco. He must have missed something important. "So tell me again, what's the problem with the little presses?"

"They're a bunch of Reds. Misfits and vermin," replied Hector. "A vagrant by the name of Luis Emilio Recabarren brought Communism to Chile."

Hector glared as if he held Luis personally responsible for Recabarren's actions. "He was nothing more than a vagrant and a misfit, with his Bolshevik press. They're all misfits and vagrants, like those Arancibia Brothers with the press out in Independencia. Right now they're promoting a strike at my father's construction site in Barrio Brasil. If it weren't for my father, those *ratos* wouldn't have work at all."

Hector was almost shouting. "Look, anything I need to read, I read in *El Mercurio*. It's published right here in Santiago by Augustin Edwards. By one of our best families. *Gente decente—*" Hector's bony face had flushed with odd patches of red. "Those Bolsheviks should be shut down right now, starting with Arancibia Brothers."

"I thought you guys were student revolutionaries."

"We're student leaders," said Hector, stiffly. "We want to work with government, not destroy it."

"What government abolishes freedom of the press?"

Things have got out of control, said Hector. What was needed was *la mano dura*. His German great-grandfather, Emil Körner, had been invited to Chile to put spine in the Chilean military. To professionalize it. Chile now had the most disciplined army in South America. But this army with its standards and discipline was being undermined by *comunistas indecentes.* Whereas the *gente decente—*

Osvaldo's words burst out of him. *"Gente decente? Qué broma!* Your father treats his cattle better than he treats his laborers at Barrio Brasil. I can't take any more of this. I'm outta here."

Santiago followed Osvaldo to the door and closed it behind the grey jacket. He shrugged. The centers of his eyebrows formed their charming, bemused little triangle above his nose. "It appears we don't interest your Marxist friend very much."

Not me either, thought Luis.

Odalís sat wide-eyed on the sofa, looking puzzled. Wefe was frowning, with her fist in her mouth. Meanwhile Hector was going on about German culture. The mining student was unusually animated. He told about spending summers at the family *fundo* in the south near Parral, near a German colony. La Colonia Dignidad. Everyone was vegetarian. They grew their own food. They were disciplined. Germans had a culture of discipline. A culture of standards. At Colonia Dignidad, men and women were sexually chaste.

The discussion of German vegetarians and their chastity was preventing Luis from hearing Del Campo and Wefe. They were chattering comfortably again in Spanish, Del Campo leaning close to her. She rubbed her thumb and forefinger up and down the stem of her wine glass, giggling. Luis could not follow their chit-chat, but he felt his blood pressure rising.

Shortly after that Odalís asked Santiago to call her a cab. She was due at the godmother's early the next morning. When the bell rang, the cousins kissed each other's cheeks— one kiss, two kisses, three. Odalís waved at the rest of them. Luis wanted to leave as well, but Wefe was enjoying herself and she ignored his signals to go.

When they finally left at midnight, Luis proposed they go on to El Bosco, a café a few blocks away. Osvaldo might be waiting for them there, with his other new friends.

Luis had met Miller Williams shortly after he arrived. The American poet from Hoxie, Arkansas, had a fellowship from Harvard and was teaching at the Universidad de Chile. He also did something with the Alliance for Progress, although it wasn't clear what.

Williams liked gossip, especially gossip which revealed an unexpected weakness or Achilles heel—which Chilean writers were secret lushes; who were addicts of various sorts; who were in the closet. He had a lot of friends. Thanks to Miller Williams, Luis was meeting all the Chilean poets. Enrique Lihn and Enrique Lafourcade. Alejandro Jodorowsky. Armando Menedín. Eliana Navarro. And the incredible Stella Diaz Varín. They were older than Luis, and they gathered almost every evening at the watering holes that lined the Alameda between U-Católica and U-Chile, places like the Café Iris and El Bosco and the Casa de las Botellas. They would be at El Bosco tonight. He would show Wefe off, and impress her with his friends, so much more sophisticated than the idiots they had just left.

As they turned onto Subercaseaux, Wefe remembered she had left her black jacket at Santiago's apartment. They were halfway to El Bosco. "Go on. Your friends are waiting. This will only take a minute. I'll meet you there." He had been stupid to believe her.

He had been welcomed with gratifying cries of "*El americano! El poeta! Mi favorito gringo!*"

He slid into a seat next to Osvaldo, ordered a Jack Daniels, lost himself in the crazy talk. Osvaldo was still steamed about the conversation on Villavicencio. His brother, Ramón, had been the Socialist student who had run against Santiago Del Campo. Ramón was convinced that Del Campo had altered the ballots. It was an old Chilean tradition—the rigged election. The young scion would have learned early how to ensure whatever outcome he wanted.

For a while Luis let himself be distracted with the conversation, but after an hour, he realized Wefe had not returned—and was not returning? Saying drunken good-byes, he stumbled back to Calle Villavicencio and rang the bell. The Belle Epoque building was dark. Silent. It seemed no one was awake (except for two people?). Luis punched the bell a second time, a third time. When there was no response, Luis held the bell down with his finger and leaned on it. Nothing.

He howled in pain, like an animal. "We-ee-ee-ee-ee-fe!" he bawled. He was wild, a mad wolf.

Silence. Total silence.

So he made his disconsolate way home through the Parque Forestal to the Avenida Condell. Could she have gone ahead without him? But in the Casa de los Falcones, Wefe's bedroom was empty.

Thus the next day's conversation.

It was unpleasant. He had accosted her in her room, sitting cross-legged on her bed, leafing through a magazine. A cigarette burned in an abalone shell on a bedside stand.

"Wefe. We have to talk."

Wefe had not looked up. "What about?"

"You know what about."

"I'm not clairvoyant. Anyway I'm reading."

"You're looking at Vogue. That's not reading."

"I don't consult with you about what I should read."

"Maybe you should."

"Please don't insult me."

"I'm not insulting you. You insult yourself."

"I'm reading an interview with Norman Mailer. In this issue of Vogue. Please don't imply I'm brainless." She was so sure of herself, this Wefe.

"I don't *imply* you're brainless." The conversation was going in a bad direction.

"Where were you last night?"

Wefe's eyes slid up and to the left. Did the answer lie in the corner of the room? "What do you mean?"

"You never showed up at El Bosco. You never came home at all. Where were you?"

"What's this third degree? You don't own me."

"I don't own you? What the fuck is that? *We have a relationship*, Wefe. We *trust each other*. You know about that? Trust? That's what people do, who love each other. They *trust each other*."

"Stop shouting at me," she said.

"I'm not shouting," said Luis, lowering his voice.

"We love each other, right?" he continued.

"Mmmmmmmm. I'm not sure."

"You're not sure? What the fuck is that? You're not sure. You told me you love me. You said, *I love you*."

"That was then."

"'That was then?--that was last week. You call that—*then*?

"Yes, I call that *then*," said Wefe. "Anyway, it's not important."

"It's not important."

"Stop repeating me. It's a small thing."

"It's a small thing? Just a small thing?"

"Stop repeating me."

"Where you were last night, that's a small thing?"

"Yes, it's a small thing. I spent the night with Santiago."

"That rotten son of a bitch."

"Actually he's extremely nice."

"It's not nice to sleep with your friend's woman."

"Well, you're not his friend—you hardly know him. And more to the point, I'm not your woman."

"So suddenly you're sleeping with that jerk? That's not a small thing, Wefe."

"Stop shouting at me. In my mind, it was a small act. You don't own me. You're fucking neurotic and jealous."

"So this is just a *small thing,*" mimicked Luis in a small, high voice. "I thought you said you love me."

"I love you, but I don't know if I *love* love you. You know what I mean? I love you, but I don't *love* love you."

"You don't *love* love me? What the fuck is that supposed to mean?" Luis hopped around, saying in a mimicky, squeaky voice, "She doesn't *love* love me. She doesn't *love* love me." He knew he appeared ridiculous, but he couldn't help himself.

"Look, I'm tired. Why don't you leave me alone."

"Are you going to sleep with him again?"

"Mmmmmmm. It just sorta happened."

"Oh, right. Just a small sorta thing."

"That's right. A small act. So now please leave. We can talk about this some other time."

So now Luis was meeting Wefe at the Plaza de Armas at three. They were meeting to hash things out, to analyze what they really meant to one another. Where it was going. Where *they* were going.

He walked to the Biblioteca Nacional and entered through the back entrance, mounting the shallow marble steps, pushing open the heavy doors. The vast vault of the library welcomed him. He often came here to work on his poems. He crossed through the reading room and gazed out at the Alameda from the enormously tall black iron grillwork of the main entrance.

He turned back through the library and exited as he had come in. At the corner of Estado and Huérfanos, a man played a sawed-off saxophone. He blew soulfully, picking up the lilt of the breeze, the tempo of the passersby. Luis recognized the melody. What Is This Thing Called Love? The saxophonist's instrument case was open. Luis pushed through the crowd and dropped in an *escudo,* as the musician blew a last, impossibly high note, which circled up, up, up into the sky and hung there.

He felt depressed. His own personal forces were out of joint.

At the Plaza de Armas Luis headed took a seat on an ornate iron bench. By three-twenty Wefe had still not shown up. At three-twenty-six, Luis saw her slim figure walking toward him. A straw bag dangled from her arm. She had on a turquoise sundress and her hair flowed like sunlight over her shoulders. She was not so much walking as she was floating, sauntering, her chin lifted, with a roll to her hips. She was a woman who was taking her time.

"You're late. It's three-thirty."

She sat down, propping her straw bag on her knees. "That's not late."

"We said three. Anyway, you look nice," he added. He slid his arm along the back of the bench.

"Thanks." She moved away.

"So what's going on with Señor Sonrisa?" His voice sounded a bit savage.

"With who?"

"You know. Señor Sonrisa. Del Campo. Your friend."

"Santiago."

"Yes. Santiago. Señor Sonrisa."

"Why are you calling him that?"

"It's a term of endearment. I'm honoring his radiant smile. His smile is like a toothpaste ad." He affected a folksy, countrified voice. "So how's he doin'?" It was totally unlike him.

"How's who doin'?"

"Señor Sonrisa. You haven't seen him?"

"Mmmmmmmm."

"Or talked to him?"

"Stop grilling me about him."

"Are you going to see him again?"

"Mmmmmmmm."

"What about us, Wefe?"

"What *about* us?"

"We have something, don't we?"

"Of course we have something. You live with us. Dad's very fond of you. You're like family." She ran her fingers over her eyelids, took a deep breath. "Remember, we talked about this before we came down here. We were going to be free to do our own thing."

Luis remembered the conversation well. At the time he had gone along, thinking mostly of his own possibilities. But now he felt desperate. He was watching the sand drip through the neck of the hourglass. There were only a few grains left. "Let's go up to Aconcagua next weekend. Spend the night in Puente del Inca and hike out to Confluencia in the morning." This was a trip Osvaldo had proposed. Luis hadn't been keen on it. It sounded like a lot of exertion. Luis preferred smoking a jay and listening to jazz.

But with Wefe? Aconcagua? The white mountain? The magic mountain? Perhaps under the blaze of its brilliant white glaciers, their love would flare again.

Wefe pulled away to look at him. "Hiking?"

"Aconcagua is incredible. The biggest mountain in the Andes. You have to see it!" He had never seen it.

"Maybe *you* have to see it. Not me."

"Okay, let's take in a flick next Saturday night. *8½*. You love Fellini. We'll go out to dinner, then catch the movie. I'll treat."

Wefe reached into the straw bag, withdrew a pack of Camels and pulled one out. She lit it and inhaled. "I can't."

"You love Fellini."

"Santiago's taking me to Viña del Mar."

A week later Osvaldo invited Luis to dinner to meet his family. The Güareís lived out in the barrio of Independencia. It was a long way out. The paved road gave way to broken old cobblestones. Tufts of grass grew where stones were missing. There were muddy puddles and potholes. Hardware stores and auto repair shops with hand-lettered signs advertising *tecno-autos, materials de demolición, ferroterías* lined the bus route. Slatted crates of bananas and melons indicated a *mercado* or a *super-mini*. Through the open window came wafts of hot metal dust and rotting fruit. Finally they got off at Avenida Rosas Salas.

Señora Güareí wiped her hands on her apron and kissed Luis on both cheeks. Her hair was skinned back from her forehead and formed a grey braid which reached to her waist. A little sister—a toddler—scampered between the chairs until *mamá* carried her into the kitchen. Osvaldo's father was powerfully built, with a strong face and bushy hair. His pants were held up with suspenders. The father told Luis he worked construction in Barrio Brasil.

While the mother prepared dinner, Osvaldo brought out a guitar. He played *la canción nueva* for Luis. *Paloma quiero contarte* and *Deja la vida volar,* songs of Victor

18

Jara. Osvaldo's voice was rough but on pitch. He was a good guitar player.

They were sitting at the table when the front door opened. Two young men pushed into the room, laughing. Osvaldo's older brother, Ramón, had prominent Indian cheekbones and a pencil-thin line of hairs above his upper lip. His friend looked like a martyr, with a high white forehead, deep-sunk eyes, black beard, shoulder-length hair. Ramón introduced his friend Jesús. The older brother grabbed an empanada from a plate and stuffed it in his mouth and offered another to his friend.

"Sit, sit, sit, sit!" said the mother, pointing to chairs.

Ramón was doubled over laughing. "Papá! *Es lucha armada!* Last night in Las Barrancas, a *momia* punched Mario Pinto in the face. Pinto's a socialist. The *momia* is a guy named Barihona. He had a pistol. Pinto's guys grabbed it and shot the *momia* in the shoulder with his own gun. Barihona's in the hospital."

The old man pounded the table. "*Muerte a las momias!*" The elder Güareí said laborers at the Barrio Brasil site wanted to strike. But a few cowards were trying to negotiate with the owners, a family by the name of Bulnes. "Bulnes is a bastard. Just like Barihona. It's all about them."

"The rich will never be on our side," said Osvaldo's mother. She hoisted the baby onto her lap. Osvaldo's baby sister sucked her thumb, staring at Luis with round little black eyes.

Luis had trouble following the excited conversation. *Momias. Fascistas. Cordones industriales. Unidad del pueblo.* It appeared the father, Ramón, and Jesús all worked at the Barrio Brasil site. "I thought your brother was a student," whispered Luis.

"He *was* a student," said Osvaldo. "He was in a technical program. But when Del Campo stole the election,

19

he and Jesús dropped out. They were disillusioned. My father got them hired on with Bulnes."

After the meal, Ramón stood up and kissed his mother's forehead. He and his friend were headed to a union meeting to discuss the *huelga*. At the door, Ramón raised his clenched fists over his head. His gaze now was low and level, and Luis felt the eyes of the young *comunista* boring into him.

"*La izquierda unida nunca será vencida.*"

"*Venceremos!*" the youths shouted and left.

The friendship with Osvaldo was a bright spot, but it was not enough. Luis was distracted, depressed by the break-up with Wefe, and spending too much time in the cafes on the Alameda. He struggled, but by the end of March, *Don Luis García* was no longer *presente*.

Chapter Two

What season was it, anyway? The seasons in Chile were all upside down. It was April, so in Berkeley it would be spring, but it was fall here in Santiago. He crossed the Alameda at Santa Rosa and walked past the Biblioteca Nacional. As he turned the corner, a few feet past him, a homeless man in a tattered jacket lay on the marble steps. His dirty hands were folded in his lap; his eyes were closed; his mouth open. As Luis passed, the man opened his eyes and held out a claw of a hand to Luis.

A man in a navy blazer and shiny tan loafers stepped by the beggar without looking. A bald man turned his tanned knob of a head but kept on walking. A young woman with an enormous red patent-leather bag pushed her baby carriage, indifferent to the claw. An oldster with a limp hustled forward. Young *tipos* with a roll to their stride walked fast past the beggar. The ice cream vendor, bicycling his push cart, called his mournful cry: *He-lada-lada-lada-lada-lada-lad-he-LA-do!* and the traffic, with its endless taxis, carts, buses and drayage, flowed down the Alameda and north up Santa Lucia.

Luis continued through the small park at the foot of Cerro Santa Lucia, past the refreshment booth with its blue-and-white awning and boxes of avocados and potatoes, chewing gum, candy bars, cigarettes, and soft drinks. He was meeting Stella Diaz Varín at the Fuente de Neptune. He no longer remembered when he first met Stella Diaz Varín. Perhaps Miller Williams had introduced them. Luis could never remember, because he felt he had always known her.

Stella Diaz Varín. Older than he was by some years—handsome, and headstrong, the center of all eyes at any gathering; tall, with milky-white skin, out-of-control red hair which streamed down her back; big breasted; strong of arm—for some reason, she had taken Luis under her wing. They had become buddies, fellow night-hawks, discussing, arguing everything, although half the time he could not follow her baritone Spanish filled with its street slang and obscenities. He would struggle for the Spanish to respond, struggling to decode her latest utterance. Then she would fix him with enormous green eyes. "Vat ees eet, Luis?" she would say, her gravelly voice expressing great tenderness. "Vat ees eet?"

"*No sé. No puedo.* I don't—I can't—" He couldn't manage the Spanish.

Cerro Santa Lucia. Tall palms swayed at the base of two branching flights of stairs, amidst a jumble of lavender-blooming hibiscus, jacarandas, kapok trees with umbrella crowns, *maitenes* with their willow-like habit; the sea-figs succulent with magenta flowers and reddish leaves; tall yellow tithonias, blue windflowers, scarlet salvia, pink oleanders with dark green leaves. Four stone lions gushed magical arcs of water into the air from their gaping jaws. Luis had a tingly sensation, against all odds, of happiness and expectation.

He climbed to the second terrace.

Two individuals had arrived before him. Santiago Del Campo and Wefe Langhorst stood watching the playful splash of the marble Cupid. They had not heard anyone come up the stairs. Wefe was staring into Santiago's eyes. She lifted her hand and placed it under his chin, drawing his face down so that he had to kiss her. Now her arm was encircling his neck, her hands clasped around his upper back. She was kissing Santiago's ear and whispering into it. Del Campo wore a yellow shirt with an open collar and khaki shorts. Black hairs sprouted on his calves. He was such a *fútbol* star.

The couple shifted now, looking forward in the same direction at the fountain with its squirting Cupid. Now

Santiago slid behind Wefe so he was standing directly behind her. He hooked his thumb into her heavy black belt, pulling her against him, saying something which caused Wefe to laugh a little too loudly.

Señor Sonrisa couldn't possibly be that amusing, thought Luis. Yet Wefe continued her throaty gurgling chuckles. In no way were these justified by Del Campo's pathetic wit, Luis was sure. Her laughter was definitely overdone. Now Señor Sonrisa had put his fingers into the front pocket of Wefe's jeans. "As if he owned her," thought Luis. Wefe's soft gurgles and overdone ha-ha-ha's irritated him. He wanted to spring forward and physically separate them. Still oblivious, the two moved off hand in hand.

Someone punched Luis on the forearm. A redhead in dark glasses, wearing an intensely green silk jacket—it was Kelly green, thought Luis—milky skin, round red strawberry lips. Pouty. A bruised strawberry. It was Stella.

Soon it was Stella and Luis who were staring at the Fuente del Neptune and the stream of water squirting from Cupid's penis. The sight led Stella to a long soliloquy—part reverie, part reminiscence, part instruction—on the various *pijos* of *hombres*. She asserted that there were a great many different shapes, sizes, and capabilities. Parra for instance was an *espada*, whereas her friend Alejandro Jodorowsky's *pijo* was shaped like a mushroom.

"Imposible! Como hongo?"

Sheila put her hand on her heart. *"Verdad! Hongo!"*

Stella made more observations on this subject, offering commentary on Enrique Lihn (cucumber), Lafourcade (carrot), and to describe her good friend, Armando Menedín, she held up her little finger. "Barely a radish," she giggled.

They climbed to the next terrace, a patio surrounding a red brick tower with medieval crenellations. There was no sign of Wefe and Santiago Del Campo. Luis was relieved. An ancient cannon three feet in length inspired Stella to more reminiscences. The cannon, she asserted, was like the *pijo* of Neruda himself—a national treasure, impressive at one time, but now too old and short to be effective.

Luis was too polite to ask about the source of her information. On the other hand, he had a pretty good idea. The entire subject was a bit off-limits and he felt some discomfort, especially when she punched him in the arm again and said, *"Et tú, Luis? Tendremos que hacer investigaciones?"*

They climbed to the top of the hill with its 360-degree view of the Andes to the east, the coastal cordillera on the west, and descended the hill on its eastern side. Halfway down was a stone moat. Narrow ledges protuded from its walls. Stella took a seat on one and removed her shoes, letting her bare feet dangle in the water. Luis sat beside her while she lit a cigarette, took a long drag, then offered it to Luis.

Stella spoke of a new literary magazine. *Epimetheus* was going to be *the* poetry magazine of Chile. A vehicle for the poetry establishment. Incidentally, the poetry establishment were all a bunch of *momias*.

"What are *momias?* " asked Luis. He remembered hearing the word at Osvaldo's.

"Mummies. The *gente decente*. They are a bore."

Epimetheus was the brain-child of the poet Miguel Serrano, who had succumbed to a fascination with Hitler. Serrano believed Hitler had been transported out of Berlin by occult forces and was alive in Antarctica. He had published his theories in a series of booklets. Despite these bizarre ideas, Don Miguel was well thought of. In fact, at the moment he was ambassador to Yugoslavia.

"You know who Epimetheus is?" Stella asked Luis.

"A Greek god?"

"A Greek god. Yes. The god of excuses!"

"No!"

"Yes!"

"Doesn't Miguel Serrano know?"

"Who knows what he knows!" She jumped down into the water; it came up to her mid-thighs. Laughing, she lifted her skirt high, bunching it around her waist. She wore no panties and Luis could see her flaming red bush. *La bandera*, he thought.

Stella picked up a stone and threw it hard against the edge of the moat. "So, Luis," she called back at him. "Did you know my *mamá* was also *gente decente?* My *mamá* owned *fundos* in Vicuña, in Santa Rita, in San Juan. Her *fundos* stretched all the way to the Argentina. But when *papá* died, the lawyers took everything. In seven years, it was all gone. I was fifteen. That's when I became a Communist."

She jumped back up and her skirt fell down around her wet thighs. "I moved to Santiago, and I became a *comunista indecente*. An indecent Communist poet. Like you, my friend."

"*No soy comunista—soy solo poeta,*" Luis clarified.

"Ah, we're all communists," she said. "Don't fight it."

They finished their descent of the *cerro*. At the foot of the hill bloomed a plant with foot-long trumpet-shaped white flowers. A guard broke one off and handed it to Stella. "*Para la bella.*"

Stella put it to her face. The thick white petal was like her milky skin. "*El floribundo,*" she said, looking up.

Avenidas De la Barra and Merced came together at the foot of the hill and still another fountain had been built there. Neptune and Aphrodite faced each other, marble folds discreetly covering their lower extremities. Stella gave Aphrodite a long gaze. "My *pechos* are bigger than hers." She gave Luis an odd sideways glance. "Shall I prove it?" she yanked her jersey down tightly, modeling her bosom.

"The evidence speaks for itself," said Luis, gallantly.

Stella turned to a forthcoming anthology of Chilean women poets. *La Mujer en la Poesía Chilena*. It would include three of her poems. "The *momias* had to include me. They wanted Christian poets like Eliana Navarro or Laura Liviano. But Neruda insisted they include me," she said, happily. "Or maybe it was Parra."

On the bridge where De la Barra changes to Loreto, they stood facing Cerro San Cristobal. Up river the axe-blade edges of the Andes were dark outlines in a grey sky. Under them flowed the mad, muddy, murky Mapucho with its furious currents and angry brown swirls. Luis wondered if the shamanic Andes had their eye on him. It was a question.

That night he saw light under the door to Wefe's room. He rapped, then pushed the door open. She was sitting on her bed, the abalone shell spilling over with butts. "What do you want?"

"Thought I'd see how you and Señor Presidente are doing. Or should I say, Señor Sonrisa."

"Why are you calling him that? Stop it."

"Have you checked out his teeth?"

"What are you talking about?"

"His big white teeth. He's a walking toothpaste ad."

"He's good-looking and you're jealous."

"Did you have a good time at the *Fuente del Neptune?*"

"You were spying on us?"

"It's a public place. I didn't know you would be there. With your new boyfriend."

"I can't believe you followed us."

"I didn't follow you. You were there. I was there. So what were you and the idiot talking about?"

"Santiago is hardly an idiot. He is one of the most intelligent men I know. He has a deep understanding of

Chile and all of its problems. That's why he ran for president of FeCH."

"And rigged the election to defeat Ramón Güareí."

"I don't believe that."

"FeCH is the tool of the government."

"No, it's not. Santiago has written to President Alessandri saying FeCH denounces the government's actions."

"Denouncing? Well, that sounds pretty heavy. What is he denouncing?"

"The government's failure to fund scholarships."

"Since when does Señor Sonrisa need a scholarship?"

"He doesn't need a scholarship. That's what's so wonderful about him. He has a big heart. He's doing this for students like your friend, Osvaldo."

"Well, congratulations to Mr. Toothpaste Ad. Doing something that doesn't benefit only himself. For once."

"You're so jealous."

"He's no revolutionary."

"Look, I'm not really in the mood for company."

"Ah, you vant to be alone." Luis faked a Garbo accent.

And so it had gone, but at the end of the conversation, it was Luis who was alone in the little maid's room which served as his bedroom. Wefe had pointedly closed her door. After a while, laughing and giggling could be heard across the hall. She was probably on the phone with him.

It was a cold afternoon at the Casa de las Botellas. Stella's fur coat was tossed over the back of her chair. Alejandro Jodorowsky was enjoying a reunion with his old friends—Enrique Lihn, Enrique Lafourcade, Armando Menedín, Stella Diaz Varín. Miller Williams was also there. Jodorowsky had been visiting his mother in Iquique and was on his way back to Mexico, or maybe it was Paris.

Jodorowsky had an expressive actor's face. He wore a black turtleneck, a heavy silver Mapuche pendant, faded jeans. There was something of the satyr about him—his tight, quick frame, the short, pointed beard. He held his eyebrows high-arched and quizzical.

Enrique Lihn had the sad, sensual face of a Roman libertine. His lips were always tasting *something*—wine, tea, *dulces*. His own words. He was Bohemian in a purple cotton shirt, baggy pants, fisherman's sandals.

The entrepreneur and publisher, Armando Menedín, was a plump little Argentine, bouncy and quick on his feet, a dandy in the best sense, a sharp dresser who had internalized the teachings of Carreño's handbook for gentlemen. Very kind, very urbane, very discreet. He would always avoid a fight or confrontation.

The poet Enrique Lafourcade had a long face topped with a pompadour of soft brown hair. He was resting his jaw on the heel of his left hand. His extended forefinger scratched the corner of his eye.

Enrique Lihn spoke. "The Communists won the popular vote in 1958. If it hadn't been for Zamorano, Allende would be President now. He stands a good chance next year. I think he'll make it."

Miller Williams, long and rangy, the country boy from Hoxie, Arkansas, drawled, "If the left gains it won't benefit Allende. The middle class will vote for the Christian Democrats. They believe reform in Chile should involve the Church. They fear the atheism of the Communist Party."

"The key," said Lihn, "has to be land reform. Chile doesn't grow enough food to feed Chileans. The *hacienda* system is broken."

"Anyone who tries to dismantle the *haciendas* will face the wrath of the *hacenderos*. They have all the money and all the political clout," objected Lafourcade.

"Look at the *callampas*. If all those people go to the polls, then the Socialist candidate will win," said Lihn. *Callampas* were shanty towns which encircled Santiago.

"They won't go to the polls. They can't read or write," said Lafourcade. "How can they vote?"

Lihn shrugged. "You see that character they're running on the right—General Abdón Barrientos? Thinks Hitler is alive somewhere in Antarctica? Believe me, a guy like him will not hesitate to organize a coup d'état. Allende's *vía pacífica* will end up *una vía sangriente*."

"Coup d'état?" said Lafourcade. "Never. We Chileans have the most stable political system in South America."

"Yes, we Chileans are the most gifted at rigging elections," said Jodorowsky, speaking for the first time.

"Kennedy's policy is to prevent the spread of Marxism by supporting democratic social reform. That's the mission of the Alliance for Progress." This was Miller Williams. "But I tell you—if a Communist gets elected? Kennedy will not allow another Cuba."

Jodorowsky put his hands over his eyes in mock horror. "My friends will lose their *becas?*"

Now they all talked at once, talking over one another, except for Jodorowsky who hummed a few bars of an old tango tune. He was bored. The other voices fell silent for a while. Then Jodorowsky raised his hand. "Politics is not a game for poets, I assure you," Jodorowsky opined gravely. "Except maybe for *la boxerena* there," he added, looking over at Stella.

She shook her fist at him. "Bring on the *momias!*"

Two or three spoons clinked against the wine glasses in forceful agreement—"Hah! Hah! Ahhh!" Grunts of assent.

Enrique Lihn leaned forward. His face was heavy, sad. "The Democratic Front would prefer to run Alessandri again, but since an incumbent president cannot succeed himself, they'll run Videla. Videla wins, then he resigns in favor of Alessandri."

Loud grunts and groans of disapproval. Former president Gabriel Gonzalez Videla had been elected in 1946 with support from the left. Pablo Neruda had been his campaign manager. Once elected, Videla outlawed the Communist Party and ordered Neruda arrested. Neruda had fled the country and remained in exile for five years. Now Videla was utterly despised by the left as a traitor.

An excited volley of voices was all speaking at once. Jodorowsky's theatrical tenor could be heard above the others. "That *hijo de puta*? May he roast in hell."

Thunderous clinking of spoons against coffee cups.

Then there was silence, and Jodorowsky picked up his tune, a popular tango ballad, Mi Noche Triste. "The song bird is at it again," said Enrique Lihn, pensively. Jodorowsky warbled several more bars. Then he too fell silent.

Luis found the politics of Chile very difficult to sort out. The Democratic Front was the most conservative coalition in Chile despite the "democratic" in its name. The Radical Party had been radical when it was founded in 1863, but one hundred years later it was controlled by a right-wing group and aligned itself with the conservative Democratic Front. Salvador Allende's Frente Acción Popular was a coalition of Communists and Socialists which appealed to intellectuals. But mainstream voters preferred the Christian Democrats.

The current president, Santiago Alessandri, had won in 1958 with only one-third of the popular vote. The left had actually received more votes, but there were two candidates competing on the left—Allende and a young Socialist priest, Antonio Zamorano. The votes cast for Zamorano cost Allende the presidency.

The 1964 presidential election was a year away, but the candidates had already announced. The Christian Democrats would be represented by Eduardo Frei. The Socialists and Communists had selected Salvador Allende, and Julio Durán was the candidate of the right-wing Democratic Front. A fourth candidate, General Abdón Barrientos, represented a small group of extremists and hard-liners whose motto was *la mano dura*.

Copper was Chile's most lucrative asset and it was controlled by two huge American mining corporations, Anaconda and Kennecott. Allende wanted to nationalize the copper industry. He also proposed to nationalize Chile's communications system, owned by the American IT&T. He wanted to restructure the enormous *latifundias* which were so inefficient that Chile imported wheat and corn from the United States. But the upper class viewed *latifundias* as their ancestral birthright and efforts to empower the working class only filled them with alarm. At the same time, the sheer number of tenant farmers and *obreros* made Allende powerful. The industrial workers, the miners, the peasants, all were joining the communist and socialist parties and sending chills of fear up the spines of *la gente decente*.

Luis was so confused by all the parties, alliances, and coalitions forming and reforming, he thought even Chileans must have a hard time sorting it out. "I thought these guys gathered to discuss poetry," he whispered to Stella.

"In Chile the poets *are* the politicians," Stella replied. "Remember? Shelley? The poets are the legislators of the race?" Then she straightened up. "Look, there's Accursio Chiarello. He talks of nothing *but* poetry."

Sitting by himself at another table a tall young man, with the most enormous beaked nose, was furiously shuffling through some papers. His black hair was pulled back into a Chinese pig-tail. Three precarious stacks of little red booklets surrounded him. He held a cigarette between the thumb and forefinger of his left hand, and a coffee cup sloshed on the table. As he worked, he puffed on the cigarette, thereby

31

spilling ashes on his papers, then slurped his coffee, with drops and slops falling every which way. Everything about him was angular and long; his long fingers were stained from nicotine, his long neck supporting the big head with its enormous beak. His skin was a sallow yellow.

"You know him?"

"Everyone knows him. Accursio Chiarello. He's one of the new food poets. They're very big right now. Especially in Argentina."

"He's not Chilean?"

"Fortunately, no. A poet from Argentina—very big. His book has just come out, *Malas Notas*. Armando speaks highly of it."

"Have you read it?"

Stella made a face.

The Argentine poet lifted his head and for a moment locked eyes with Luis. Then he looked away.

"Come on," said Stella. "I'll introduce you."

The gangly bird welcomed them, sweeping his papers into a pile to make room for them. In doing so, he knocked his cup over. Brown liquid ran over his manuscript in a long spreading flow with coffee-colored tributaries. It was a miniature Rio de la Plata. Stella introduced Luis as an American poet.

"Ah, a Pen-Rod," said the Argentine. He exaggerated the word, separating the two syllables. Then Accursio immediately asked whether Luis considered himself a surrealist or a formalist.

"A surrealist," said Luis.

"No. Surrealism is miserabilism. It's dead. A poet has to demonstrate that he can work in the form. Sonnets. Villanelles. Rhymed quatrains. Either you can do it, or you can't." His bulging eyeballs mocked Luis. "You take your sestina. Invented by Arnaut Daniel in the twelfth century, picked up by Petrarch and Dante, not to mention your American, Ezra Pound. Really old form, with hundreds of years of history. I've had a go at it. Maybe I could read to you my Jubileo en Jujuy. It's in rime royale."

"Or the villanelle? Ever write a villanelle?" Accursio didn't wait for an answer. "I have one called Llullaillaco Villanelle."

The sound came out: Jhoo-jhai-jhacko.

"They're both in here," said Accursio, patting one of the red books. *Malas Notas* was inscribed in gold letters on the spine.

"So what *is* the meaning of art?" Accursio asked. His bulging eyeballs seemed to hold Luis captive. This guy is crazy, Luis thought to himself. He careens from one subject to another. What is art? But in the spirit of the conversation, Luis tried to formulate his thoughts.

"To me," he offered, "sonnets, sestinas, that formalism stuff—that's putting a metronome on the music. You get a dead beat. You remove the phrasing, the nuance."

The Argentine looked at him with eyebrows raised.

"But in surrealism, you're in the dream, and the dream is where the images come from. Through dreams, or maybe drugs, you go way down inside yourself and find a reality you never expected. Images which are not banal. Then you set these to music—not literally to music, but to the music inherent in the language." Not a bad answer, thought Luis; but Accursio was shouting at him in a loud voice.

"*Go way down?* I don't want to *go way down*—what?—and discover I'm in love with my mother? Naaah," sneered Accursio. "Formalism is required to give sense and meaning to chaos."

"Look," said Luis. "Poetry isn't some some a-b-a-b-c-d-c-d thing. Who gives a fuck about rhyme? That's kindergarten jingles. *Little Miss Muffet sat on a tuffet?* I'd much rather let the chaos in."

"May I?" said Accursio, but he didn't wait for permission.

He read his Taco Sonata. It wasn't bad. In a rather formal way, using the dreaded a-b-a-b-c-d-c-d rhyme scheme, the poem welcomed Mexican street food into the repertoire of Argentine cooking.

Accursio treated Luis and Stella to more of his views. He had views on modernism, post-modernism, futurism, formalism, neo-realism, and a whole host of other -isms, including his favorite -ism, kitchen-ism, or *cocinismo,* the "food poetry" by which he planned to emblazon the name Chiarello in the annals of mid-to-late twentieth century poetry.

Stella rolled her eyes.

"Have you heard my latest poem, La Empanada Final?" Accursio's long, cigarette-stained fingers were turning over the pages of his *Malas Notas* rapidly.

"Not now, Accursio," groaned Stella, covering her ears with her hands. Her red nail polish was chipped. "Surprise us later, darling."

"Well, I have another one," said Accursio. "May I?" And without waiting, he declaimed Noche de los Nachos. This poem took the lowly Mexican burrito as an image of the little donkey on which the Virgin entered Bethlehem. In a brilliant turn, one of the Three Wise Men was revealed to be a shaman from the Altiplano whose gifts to the newborn Messiah included melted queso on corn tortillas, an avocado dip, and three *hongos mágicos.*

"Cool, man," said Luis.

"Okay, read me one of yours."

Luis read a poem he was working on.

Alone upon an empty playground,
I became a lion:
keen-eyed, muscled and
fast to leap.
And in the waving grove,
among rivers of
diffuse light,
shadows turned to tiny grey sparrows,
and violet humming birds
flew
at my glance.

"Cool, *hombre*," said Accursio. He seemed truly appreciative. And in this way they became friends and met often to discuss what is art and to read one another their poems.

Luis had been in Santiago three months when Miller Williams proposed they visit Nicanor Parra in La Reina. Luis knew Parra's poems from the City Lights Pocket Poets edition. In fact, he had a question for Parra about one of his poems, but Parra was rarely found in the cafés and watering holes along the Alameda. He taught mathematics at the Universidad de Chile and when he wasn't teaching, he was at his casita way out in the barrio of La Reina, on Santiago's easternmost edge. Luis had wondered if there would ever be an opportunity to meet him. Now, thanks to Miller Williams, it was happening. At Plaza Egaña, the cab driver headed straight out Avenida Larraín toward the Andes. When the road ended, they turned left onto a sandy lane, Avenida Alvaro Casanova, and climbed into the hills.

Miller Williams knocked. After a while a barefoot woman with long black hair appeared at the door. She looked at them without saying a word, then padded away, slim ankles visible beneath the white hem of her skirt. She returned in a moment with Parra himself.

Parra was fifty years old. His curly black hair sported two white shafts at the temples. He looked exactly like what he was—a distinguished Chilean-European intellectual. Enormous vitality exuded from his person. He led them toward the back of the house to an outdoor patio. It was an oasis in the dry landscape. An enormous *maitén* tree, its drooping branches resembling a willow, shaded a round table. Purple plums had fallen on the warm flagstones of the patio, giving off a sweet fermented scent.

The sun was hot. Luis could smell the arid slopes of the foothills, which mixed the camphor of eucalyptus, the scent of dry grass, and the smell of soil. Occasional clumps of dark pine scrub dotted the yellow hills. Zig-zagging gullies which had channeled winter rains had left trail-like traces. The landscape resembled California but with something more brutal in it. Rising in the background were the dark axe-blade shapes of the Andes.

Luis remembered the summer he was fourteen, spent in his grandfather's library in Redlands. Louis Mertins had been a poet himself and a friend of Robert Frost's. Breezes blew in the open windows while Luis read Frost and Walt Whitman and Robinson Jeffers. At fourteen Luis already knew he was a poet, a poet who had not yet written his poems. Later, trying to understand his Spanish heritage, he devoured García Lorca and Luis Cernudo and the writers and artists of La Residencia in Madrid, and the little Pocket Poets *Anti-Poems of Nicanor Parra.*

> *We do not speak*
> *solely to be heard*
> *But so others may speak*
> *And the echo precedes the voice that produces it.*

and,

> *What I say is, let's try to be happy*
> *Sucking on the miserable human rib,*
> *Let's extract from it the restorative liquid,*
> *Each one following his own personal inclinations.*
> *Let's cling to this divine table scrap.*

Now Luis had arrived. Reality was heightened. Reds were more red. Greens were greener. The sunlight in the patio was gold, cream, almost tactile. The *maitén* tree was alive, listening, and little birds hopping in its branches were alert and paying attention. He was inhabiting his fate. All things were possible.

"Poetry, like energy, can neither be created, nor destroyed," Parra said. "Just as there is anti-matter, so there is also anti-poetry." In anti-poetry, *nadie* is *todo*. No one is everyone. Poems must root themselves in common speech—slangy, informal, colloquial—and reflect daily life. And it was important not to take poetry too seriously. "The problem with Pablo Neruda? Everytime he writes a poem, he thinks he's praying ," said Parra. "You see, Luis? Nothing is sacred."

Miller Williams jumped in to read his translation of Parra's *Montaña Rusa:*

> *For half a century*
> *poetry was the paradise*
> *of the solemn fool.*
> *Until I came along*
> *and built my roller coaster.*
>
> *Go up, if you feel like it.*
> *It's not my fault if you come down*
> *With your mouth and nose bloody.*

"So is there any place for formalism in poetry? Villanelles, sestinas, sonnets? Doesn't that formal structure get in the way?" asked Luis.

Parra laughed. "Do you know my Jovenes poem?"

> *Write as you will*
> *In whatever style you like.*
> *In poetry, everything is permitted,*
> *With only this condition of course,*
> *You have to improve on the blank page.*

"Yes, but you don't write in those old forms. Your poems are like crossword puzzles. Witty, unexpected. Modern. No rhyme at all. You get a rhythm, but not by using rhyme. Aren't I right?" Luis persisted.

"Well, look," responded Parra. "Rhythm. Rhyme. They're the same word, really. Take the *th* out of rhythm, and you've got rhyme. You don't like rhyme's sing-song quality, but the predictability makes it easy to memorize, and it's soothing to the listener. It's characteristic of children's lullabies and folk ballads."

"But who is writing lullabies and folk ballads now?" Luis had to get this straight. "This return to the forms of the Middle Ages—sestinas, villanelles, etc.—isn't it pretentious?"

"Not so long as you improve upon the blank page," laughed Parra.

"I have another question," said Luis. He opened his City Lights Pocket Poets *Anti-Poems*. "In your poem The Tunnel—the three *tías*. Are these aunts mythical figures?"

"No, no, no, no—they really existed—at least, two of them did. I was teaching in Chillán and my fiancée invited me to meet her parents in Coihueco. I planned to take the train. Her family was rich and I wasn't sure they would accept a poor young teacher as a son-in-law, and I couldn't sleep. I feared her family would reject me as a son-in-law. Then I had an idea. I would get off the train one stop ahead and hire a small carriage to take me the rest of the way. The family would be waiting for me to get off the train. Arriving in my private *cochecito,* I would appear to be a young man of means."

"The *cochecito* made a stop in Paso de Piedra and there a school teacher friend asked a favor—could I give a lift to his two aged aunts? They were in danger of missing their train. My friend didn't wait for my answer before he was loading the aunts into my *cochecito,* along with three boxes of watermelons. As we pulled up to the train station in Coihueco, my love and her family were waiting for me. But I had to help the old ladies down, and as I unloaded the boxes of watermelons, they spilled all over the ground, and I was running after them and picking them up, looking more like a porter than a young man of means. The family greeted me very coldly. But the very coldest of all was Maruja."

"That was the turning point," laughed Parra. "I knew if I married Maruja, I would be set up for life. Her family was *gente decente* with a big *fundo*. But maybe it was running after the watermelons. She wouldn't look at me, she wouldn't sit next to me. I realized if I married her I would be trading all my freedom for the values of those *burgüesas*. I ran like hell," said Parra, laughing his belly laugh.

"I got back on the train I'd come out on. That's when I wrote The Tunnel."

> *A young man of meager means is hardly aware of most*
> *   things.*
> *He lives in a glass bell called Art, Called Sex, called Science,*
> *Trying to get in touch with a world of elements*
> *Which only exist for him and a small group of friends.*

"I was saved!" laughed Nicanor and he waggled his black eyebrows.

Now and again the dark-haired woman passed through the patio, bringing fresh pitchers of sangría, plates of cheeses and persimmons. She was so beautiful. But so silent. Was she a servant? Was she Nicanor's wife? Parra did not introduce her.

At the end of the afternoon, the cab let him off at the Biblioteca Nacional, but Luis did not enter its vaulted reading room. He walked home through the Parque Forestal. His head was filled with memories of the scents and odors of the afternoon, Parra's deep laugh. Luis was still in thrall to that heightened reality which he had felt in Parra's presence. At the same time, heading toward La Casa de los Falcones, he was sad. Wefe would not be home. She had turned elsewhere.

Between Pio Nono and Puríssima he stopped to gaze at the Fuente Alemana. A huge bronze male, half-naked, was pinned to a sail. Perhaps he was Odysseus passing the Sirens. Behind him spread the enormous metallic wings of a condor. A plaque stated the bird represented the Chilean *raza*. *Raza*—an odd word for a population of Mapucho, Aymara, Quechua, Spanish, Basque, English, German, Welsh. The bronze had been donated to the city of Santiago by the Colonia Alemana. Was the Colonia Alemana thinking of only one *raza*? Its own?

It was cold and Luis pulled up his collar. It was April— so soon it would be summer. No, wait a minute. What season was it anyway? Soon it would be winter. It was already fall.

40

Chapter Three

Luis often finds himself in El Bosco, having a *cafecito* and waiting for Stella. It is a dark bar with small tables and a few booths, across the Alameda from the Iglesia de San Francisco. The bar is popular with students, poets, artists, and intellectuals. Although El Bosco is barely two blocks from the Biblioteca Nacional, Luis begins to avoid the Biblioteca, with its air of massive importance, in favor of this hole in the wall where he feels he can be more himself.

"Me encuentro en un bosco oscuro," Luis says to himself in Spanish. The thought has formed in his new language and floats in his head. Lost in the dark bowels of El Bosco, Luis himself is a Dante, although not exactly in the middle of his life's journey. In fact, he has barely embarked on it. But he is tormented by dangers that appear to lurk on all sides. He has a dream. He is peering down a deep well. It is the sacred well at Chartres, an ancient Druidic well, with dark powers. At the bottom is Wefe's face, staring back up at him. She seems confused, lost and alone. He tries to reach for her, but the distance of the well spans centuries. He is falling forward. Finally his fingers touch her face and in that moment, the image breaks apart.

He is a poet—that is the one certainty. He works hard on his poems. His minimal utterances. Minimal though they might be, they require all of his effort. He must screw his effort to the sticking point. Hamlet. Or was that Macbeth?

Wefe's new love affair worries Luis. He has seen Del Campo with another woman from a distance. Del Campo's arm had been around the girl's waist. Luis mentions this sighting to Wefe. She shrugs. She and Santiago don't own each other. She doesn't tell Santiago whom he can and cannot see. They are like Jean-Paul Sartre and Simone de Beauvoir.

Wait a minute. He, *Luis*, is Jean-Paul Sartre. Has Wefe forgotten? Comparing that idiot Santiago with Sartre is insulting to him, Luis, but it is also troubling. Does she truly see Señor Sonrisa in such grand terms? Wefe is giving Luis up for a romancer, a womanizer, and a political fraud. Then Wefe strikes a woman-of-the-world pose. If she is a fool, so what? Life is short. (She is twenty-two, Luis reflects.) Anyway, there *is* no meaning to life. It makes absolutely no difference. She starts wearing a black beret, pulling it down so that her blonde hair cascades out of it, and smoking Gauloises. She reads *Nausea*.

Everyone asked such unanswerable questions. What was art? What was the meaning of life? He Luis was in the middle of a dark woods. He didn't have any answers.

His moment of truth would come soon, at the end of June, when the left-leaning poets—who were most of them— were giving a big reading at the Café Iris. Armando Menedín was organizing the event to draw attention to his *Ediciones Renovación*, his poetry series being printed by Arancibia Hermanos. The line-up was impressive: Nicanor Parra (who would have to leave early for a Festschrift in honor of a retiring astronomer); Enrique Lihn; Enrique Lafourcade; Alejandro Jodorowsky; Stella Diaz Varín; Eliana Navarro. Armando had asked Accursio Chiarello and Luis García to read a few poems at the end to demonstrate the talent of the younger set.

The evening of the reading the Café Iris was jammed. All the poets were there with their friends, fans, foes, and on-lookers. Luis saw Osvaldo, who had brought Ramón and Jesús. Wefe and Santiago Del Campo were there. Hector Körner Bulnes and the pretty little Odalís. It was a full house.

Luis and Stella sat at a table near the stage. Luis watched a man push his way toward them. He had a long torso and short, strong legs. A black-and-white striped polyester shirt hung out from under his dirty jacket. "Who's that?" Luis asked Stella.

"Oh, shit, it's my husband," she said.

Tito Bustos had thick labial folds and a five o'clock shadow. He was an ox. With him, hanging slightly back, was a *tipo* with a skinny butt. Despite the cold, the young man was wearing only a thin T-shirt. Dark, furtive. He stood with a fixed gaze, staring off at something far away. His leg was jiggling; his foot tapping. Whatever was on his mind, it wasn't here.

Tito Bustos leaned over Stella's chair and said something to her. When he opened his mouth, an aluminum tooth was visible in his upper jaw. Then he laughed, a bad laugh, in his nose. And the two men left.

Stella looked angry.

"Who was that guy with your husband?" asked Luis.

"A piece of scum named Chico Silva."

"What did they want?"

"Nothing," said Stella. She wasn't talking.

The evening began. A Mapuche singer chanted about an owl who goes, *Tukuu, tooo-kooooo. Tucu, nuco, nucurutu.* The Mapuche was followed by a violinist, a flautist, and a drummer. The trio was dressed up in blue feathered head-dresses, cuffs at the ankles with little bells. They had smeared designs of white and blue clay on their dark skin to resemble Aymara warriors. Although the Aymara warriors with feathers and bells had lost to Spaniards with *pistolas*, the crowd was delirious with these reincarnations of Chile's indigenous heritage. The trio shouted their songs, invoking the vast spaces of the Altiplano. Everyone was clapping in unison.

Then the poets. Nicanor Parra read first. He read Montaña Rusa, El Tunel, and La Vibora. Enrique Lihn read from his book, *Recuerdos del Matrimonio*. His Roman libertine face was sad. The marital *recuerdos* were *tristes*. Enrique Lafourcade ran his hand nervously over his pompadour. "*El pasado, la future—dos muertes. Solamente el presente—eso es vida,*" he declaimed, from his *Invención a Dos Voces*. Miller Williams read from his manuscript, *Halfway from Hoxie,* translating the originals into Spanish on the spot and adding ad-libbed improvements in an Arkansas drawl. Stella read from her *Sinfonía del Hombre Fossil*. Eliana Navarro read a poem about the Mother of God.

Alejandro Jodorowsky took his time. First he hauled two boards onto the stage. They had been fashioned into a cross. Then he nailed a dead chicken to it. Two women mounted the stage, attacking the mutilated chicken with their fingernails. Jodorowsky screamed, "The Apocalypse is now! Our only hope is the flying saucers!" This bizarre offering was greeting with an outpouring of applause.

To round out the first part of the evening, Armando had imported two tango performers from Buenos Aires to dance to the mournful tunes of the *milonga*. After several minutes of stylized spins, dips, and turns, the male dancer stepped back, and the woman dancer, wearing a tight black skirt and impossibly high heels, held out her arms to the audience. She was inviting a male to partner her.

Accursio unfolded himself and took his place on the stage, drawing himself up to his full height and assuming an expression of arrogant hauteur. He wore a flat black sombrero, a white flowing scarf at the neck; baggy pantaloons tucked into high-heeled boots; and, when he turned his back, the audience could see the ornate gaucho knife tucked into his waistband. For such an uncoordinated individual, he proved adept, his feet always moving to the right spot to avoid his partner's flirty little tango kicks. At the end, in a daring step, the female dancer lifted one thigh and wrapped her leg around his waist. With an impassive and cold face, Accursio bent her into the long parabola of a backbend, while the musicians played a pause note. The crowd clapped vigorously, and Accursio resumed his seat.

Then it was the break and the tango woman joined Accursio at his table, embracing him in the Argentine style. Kiss one, kiss two, kiss three. Right cheek, left cheek, right. Apparently they already knew each other.

Luis was nervous. This would be his first reading in Santiago, to a crowd who did not know him. He glanced around. Several tables over Wefe leaned forward, her chin on her hands. She was so lovely with her swan neck and delicate jaw line. Wherever she was, light pooled around her. Del Campo's tanned arm lay on the back of her chair, the fingers of his other hand drumming the table restlessly. Luis felt rage surge in him. How could he perform, feeling such anger? Then he saw how he could use this rage for his reading. He would punch Del Campo out with his syllables. The thought galvanized him.

Armando Menedín walked over to Accursio. "We could put García up now."

"The *gringo* can read when I'm finished."

"The best is always last. Let him warm up for you."

"Pen-Rod is reading his stuff in English. Everyone will leave. Why should I read to an empty house?"

"Almost every poet in this room understands English."

"I'll go next," insisted the Argentine.

So now came the turn of Accursio Chiarello. He stood bathed in a spotlight, six feet six inches of him, with his long beak of a nose and weak chin. His black hair was pulled back in a pony-tail. Despite his dashing gaucho get-up, he resembled a gigantic stork—not the kind that brings babies in a blanket, but the kind that eats them. In his hands was his little red book, his *Malas Notas*.

Accursio led off with the Taco Sonata. He had a long

tongue, like a lizard's. It flitted in and out of his mouth, licking his words. He had an irritating lisp when he was rattled, not that he was rattled tonight; he was reading his best stuff, but the lizard tongue was tripping him up, it was darting here and there. Accursio moistened his lips, but his words sounded thick, with lisping s's and thickened y sounds.

"*Tiene voz de palta,*" murmured Stella. It was true Accursio's Argentine accent crushed the castellano *y's* and double *ll's* as thoroughly as a cook smashes a ripe avocado into guacamole.

The tango woman flung her long brown hair back and narrowed her eyes at them. "*Callate. Vos!*" she snarled.

Accursio ripped into the Tortilla Suite in three parts: Desayuno, Almuerzo, and Snacks. He read Jubileo en Jujuy, in rime royale, working in *ojos* (eyes); *joyas* (jewels); *jugos* (juices), *juegos* (games), *junglas* (jungles), *Jauja* (a mythical city of irrepressible happiness pronounced *how-ha*), and the *hoo hoo* sounds of a train's whistle. Suddenly his lisp was no problem. Jubileo en Jujuy was a tour de force. Accursio followed with a softly-spoken, almost whispered, Llullaillaco Villanelle. One could have heard a pin drop. The audience was then treated to Noche de los Nachos, linked to the life of Christ, who eats a final, fatal empanada. Next he tore into his sonnet, Alfajore, Mi Amore, addressed to the famous Argentine pastry. The tango woman was waving and clapping hysterically. "Accursio! Accursio!"

"Maybe she's the *alfajore*?" whispered Stella.

Accursio was winding up with the title poem from *Malas Notas*. The poem was a literary fable, a veiled allusion, describing the hated figure of the right, General Abdón Barrientos, comandante of the First Army Division in Antofagasta. Yet others argued that Accursio sympathized with Barrientos, and the poem was in fact a paean to the general. The poem's metaphors were so confusing, its ambiguities so impenetrable, when heard in this wine-flooded, smoke-filled setting, that although the audience was thrilled to be "in the know," no one could be confident of what exactly was "known." At length Accursio stood down to gratifying applause. "*El porteño! El porteño*," the audience shouted, *porteño* being the term for those from Buenos Aires.

Accursio was sure his reading had earned him the respect of the two Enriques, both Lihn and Lafourcade, of Jodorowsky, and of Nicanor Parra himself who would be unable to resist and would have to join in the tsunami of praise for him, Accursio.

Now it was Luis's turn. He perched on a tall stool under the spotlight, lay his black snap binder on his knees, and opened to the first poem. For a second, he thought of Del Campo, and felt his anger turn to pure energy.

"The Cellist," he intoned.

His voice surprised him. Where was this sound coming from? He himself was the cello, seeking and finding raw, delicious, profound notes. He was channeling Janos Starker, the poem had become his own personal unaccompanied cello suite.

Then he read The Butterfly Downed in the Inkwell, his homage to García Lorca. His voice went loud. Then *very* soft. Thundering, filling the room with *sonidos de inglés;* then whispering. Accursio had been good. Luis was even better. Poem after poem—in English, not Spanish—Lines at an Intersection, That Was a Garden Once, The New Words, That Small Act.

Tinkling, chanting, growling, groaning. He was channeling Monk, he was channeling Coltrane, he was channeling Mingus. He was a saxophone, honking, howling, squealing his high notes, screaming his vision. The room erupted in shouts and cheers, two times, three times louder than the applause for Accursio. Fists pounded tables, glasses were struck with spoons, feet stamped the floor. People were berserk with excitement. *"El gringó! El gringó!" El gringó!"* The audience accented the last syllable in a pounding rhythm.

Accursio watched with horror.

Luis was wrapping up with The Calculated Lion. The *americano* was snarling like a tiger, babbling like a monkey, jeering like a hyena, and in his last lines roaring like the king of the jungle itself. Where did García get this?

Accursio slinks away like Iago in *The Merchant of Venice*, vowing revenge. To be upstaged like this by the *gringo*. This could not stand. This could not be. But he would not reveal his heart to anyone.

The next day Luis and Miller Williams made another visit to Avenida Alvaro Casanova. Soon they were sitting under the enormous *maitén* tree with Parra. The silent woman walked barefoot on the flagstones, bringing *sangría* and empanadas. Luis leaned back, enjoying the the screech and chirp of little birds in the *maitén*. He was basking in a sense of something well done. Wefe had come up to him after the reading and kissed him. "You were fantastic!" she had said, her grey eyes shining.

"Too bad you couldn't stay, Don Nica," Miller Williams was saying. "It was an amusing evening."

"How was Jodorowsky's performance?" asked Parra.

"You call a performance nailing a dead chicken to a cross while a couple of half-dressed women scratch it with their fingernails? Jodorowsky has nothing to offer. He's a complete egotist."

"An egotist, but an interesting one. Although sometimes I fear for his sanity," said Parra.

Miller Williams turned to Luis. "But this young man stole the show last night. The Argentine poet was somewhat entertaining. But García brought down the house."

Luis allowed himself to beam for a moment before he spoke. "Nicanor, you fear for Jodorowsky's sanity. I sometimes fear for my sanity. Working on a poem, I feel like I'm staring down into a deep well. The poems lie somewhere over that abyss. If I reach for them, I may fall over. It scares me." Luis thought of the dark woods which was his life. There were dangers and abysses on all sides. One misstep? One pitfall?

One pratfall? Nicanor's twinkling eyes seemed to be saying. His black eyebrows wiggled up and down. "You must become a friend of ambiguity, my friend. Not all equations balance. Allow the poems to be unknowns for a while. Do as much as you can, then open your hand. When it is time, they will fall into your hand, like Eve's apples. So show me."

Luis opened his book bag, pulling out the black snap binder. He had a dozen or so poems typed on onion skin paper. Parra reached for reading spectacles. Birds chattered in the *maitén* tree with a raspy note, metal scraped over metal. The day was warm and breezy. Parra took his time. Finally he slapped the pages down on the table. "You're a poet, García!" His broad smile made the corners of his eyes crinkle. He read aloud Luis's A Morning in Santiago:

> *I want to carve faces*
> *with hard lips*
> *that speak of the green scent*
> *of a cool wind*
> *or of the rain's*
> *intricate writing on windows;*
> *mouths that celebrate*
> *with song the luxury*
> *of blowing oaks;*
> *or tell even a little*
> *of the sea's bells ringing red.*

49

"Call Armando Menedín." Parra scribbled a number on a piece of paper. "Tell him I said to make you a book. These should be part of his *Ediciones Renovacion.*"

Luis leaned back. He felt calm, yet excited. He could even understand the raspy conversation of the birds. They were squawking *Luisito! Luisito! Poeta! Poeta!*

And in this way, Luis's career was launched.

A week later Luis and the plump Argentine took a taxi out to Avenida Coronel Alvarado 2602. Armando Menedín told Luis the story of the Arancibia Hermanos—two Catalan brothers who had fled the Spanish civil war. Pablo Neruda had paid for their passage, and the passage for many others, on the good ship Winnipeg. It had arrived in Valparaiso in 1939.

It was a long ride out past toward Hippodrome on a wet, cloudy winter day. As the taxi hurtled over bumpy cobblestones and potholes, Luis recognized Osvaldo Güareí's neighborhood. It was the same desolate zone of *ferroterías, talleres metálicos, tecno-autos* which Luis had visited four months earlier. *Venta materials de demolición.* A block past Rosas Salas, Avenida Coronel Alvarado broke into two sections, joining with Avenida Luis Galdames. The Taller Gráfico Arancibia Hermanos at 2602 faced a triangle of hardened earth with wispy yellowing grass. The racket of the Mergenthaler Linotype machine clanked within. After several knocks, Max Arancibia opened the door.

He had a long bony face with near-set Modigliani eyes, but his expression brightened when he saw his guests. Menedín introduced Luis. So this was the printer that Hector Körner Bulnes wanted to shut down, Luis thought. Max Arancibia, despite his look of depression, seemed very gentle. Luis had *The Calculated Lion* manuscript ready for him. Armando explained he wanted *The Calculated Lion* included in his *Ediciones Renovación.* When might Max be able to print one hundred copies? Max had another job he would be doing at the time of the Fiestas Patrias—*Sangrientas Luchas de los Obreros Chilenos*.

The bloody battles of the Chilean workers. The title would horrify Hector Körner Bulnes, Luis thought. Maybe Max Arancibia read his face, because he addressed Luis.

"What does Marx say? The workers must seize the means of production? We ensure our freedom of the press when we are the press. The Chilean Communist Party was founded by a press man, Luis Emilio Recabarren. An honorable and hard-working man who went to prison many times for speaking out. *El Mercurio* reports the problem is labor—it makes ridiculous demands. Its owner, Augustín Edwards, is not interested in the condition of the workers."

It was agreed that Arancibia Hermanos would print one thousand copies of *Sangrientas Luchas* the morning of Thursday, September 19th, and one hundred copies of *The Calculated Lion* would be printed later that day.

The late afternoon was wet and cold, but El Bosco was steamy as Luis pushed open the door, noisy with a clatter of cups and crockery, a gossipy buzz, bursts of hah hah hah's! People were bundled up for winter and squeezed into the warm space. An infant squealed; Luis could hear the papa's sharp "*Cállate!*" The light of a hanging lamp reflected as a yellow oval in the window. He ordered a coffee with brandy.

The front door kept opening and closing. Each time the cold wind blew in a few more figures. Stella entered, her red hair flowing over her old fur coat. Luis waved and pointed to an empty chair at his table.

She slid into the seat, unfastening her fur. "What are you drinking, Luisito?"

Luis passed her his cup. "I'm celebrating! Armando is going to include *The Calculated Lion* in his series! It was Parra's suggestion. My book will come out in September."

"Fantastic!" said Stella. "Say, will you stand me one of those." Luis motioned to the waiter, pointed to his cup, held up two fingers.

At a table nearby Enrique Lihn, Enrique Lafourcade, and Miller Williams were engrossed in conversation. Alejandro Jodorowsky stood behind them, juggling three oranges, tossing and catching them, as the others talked. He always had one or two in the air. Miller Williams was interrogating Jodorowsky.

"Are you a Communist? Or a Socialist?"

"I am a hybrid—both human and animal," said Jodorowsky. "Therefore, an anarchist." The oranges flew into and out of his hands. "There is no government for someone like me. Art has its own laws. Those are the only laws I obey." The oranges were sailing over his head in dizzying orbits.

"So you don't believe in government?" Miller could be so square at times. So Hoxie, Arkansas, thought Luis.

"People need art, they need philosophy," Jodorowsky replied, catching an orange, and sending it flying again. "They don't need government."

"How are you going to bring art and philosophy to the people if the people can't read?" asked Miller Williams.

"Believe me, *amigo,* I can fill any plaza in Chile. I'll put two naked women on the stage and announce my play. Filosofía para Todos. I assure you everyone will come listen to my philosophy." Jodorowsky caught each of the oranges one by one and placed all three on the table.

"And while they're gaping at the ladies, I'll go around with my top hat," and here he whipped out his cap and held it upside down, shuffling and scraping, approaching each person in turn, whimpering haltingly in a high squeaky voice: "*Escudos? Escudos, señores? Escudos por la revolución?*" He made his voice break pathetically. Very high-pitched.

Miller looked unconvinced   Something about Jodorowsky confounded the Arkansan. They were two such different figures—Miller in his plaid shirt and thinning hair, such an earnest American. And the magician, fox-like and quick, with glittering eyes and pointed, satyr-like beard. Even slightly demonic.

"*No soy surrealista. Soy paniquista!* You've heard of the Panic movement, *amigo?*"

"Panic? What are you scared of?" Williams could be so Hoxie. So un-hip.

"Boredom, *señor*. Ever think of that? Why prevent me from dying of hunger if I'm just going to die of boredom?" Jodorowsky picked up an orange and lobbed it back over his shoulder, then twirled and caught it. "The Panic movement— it's the god Pan, *hombre*. Half animal. Half human. Impossible? Because Pan can't be explained?   That's Pan, and he's at the center of our movement."

The magician sighed. "Oh, you *comunistas*, you *socialistas!* You are so serious. You are so very, very humorless. We *paniquistas* embrace all that is mysterious— and all that is absurd."

"Your Panic movement is not going to work for Chile," said Miller Williams. He sounded angry. "Don't be stupid. Chile needs educators. Teachers."

"What Chile needs is an alchemist, *hombre*.   To turn Chile's shit into gold." And collecting all his oranges, Jodorowsky sat down and hid behind a big newspaper.

Miller Williams was sputtering.   After a moment Jodorowsky lay the paper down. He was trying to suppress a laugh. "*La boxerena,*" he called out to Stella. "I need your *mano dura*. I need protection. I think Mister Williams wants to punch me out."

Stella grabbed her fur and lurched between crowded tables to join the poets. Through the smoky air Luis made

53

out Accursio Chiarello's elongated figure against the wall. He was leaning back, his eyelids closed. Luis picked up his drink and his coat and joined the Argentine. "Hey, man."

Accursio did not open his eyes. "Pen-Rod. *Que pasa?*"

"I was out at Arancibia Hermanos this afternoon."

Accursio's eyelids opened to narrow slits. "What were you doing out there?"

Luis meant to sound nonchalant, but a note of pride crept into his tone. "I was delivering my manuscript."

Accursio sat up now, his eyes fixed on Luis. "They're doing a book for you?"

"Armando is going to include my book in his *Ediciones Renovación.*" Despite his attempt at nonchalance, pride peppered each syllable.

Accursio frowned so ferociously his black eyebrows merged into his nose. His left eye—the one staring at Luis—was a Picasso eye, somehow misplaced on his profile, and not happy. There was not a young poet in Santiago who did not want his book printed by the Arancibia Brothers. But Max Arancibia had rejected *Malas Notas.* To disguise his conflicted emotions, Accursio took refuge in a solicitous tone. It failed to conceal the jeer. "Well, congratulations. And so when is this little *librito* going to come out?"

Luis was too euphoric to care about the belittling *librito*. "Fiestas Patrias. Max will run my book after he prints *Sangrientas Luchas de los Obreros Chilenos.*"

"*Sangrientas Luchas de los Obreros*? Sure sounds like Marxist propaganda to me," said Accursio. "But, hey. Congratulations. *Súper, hombre.*"

Accursio was consumed with a raging jealousy. It almost blinded him. In his head, gears and bells and whistles and levers clanged together, like a mad Ferdinand Leger painting come to life, a Mergenthaler Linotype machine clanking out terrible, atonal music. He could care less about politics—left or right. But revenge. He was not the spiritual heir of Macchiavelli for nothing.

"So how's the *cocinismo*?" asked Luis.

Accursio tried to ignore the clanking rhythms in his head. He pulled himself together. "Fantastic. Miguel Serrano accepted the Tamale Sonata for his new magazine. *Epimetheus.*"

"I thought it was the Taco Sonata," said Luis.

"I'm doing a triptych. The Taco Sonata. The Tamale Sonata. And then the Tostada Sonata."

"No Ballad of the Burger? How about Hymn to the Hotdog? Or Canción a lo Ketchup?" This was a little payback for the *librito*.

"Are you making fun of me?"

The two poets locked eyes.

A tap on Luis's shoulder broke the tense moment. Osvaldo, Ramón, and Jesús were pulling up chairs. Osvaldo was carrying his guitar case. "We've just come from the *huelga*," he said. We've closed down Bulnes' construction site. Well, it's a stop-work for now, but we're drawing up demands. So what's up with you?"

Luis described his visit to the Arancibia Brothers.

Osvaldo slapped him on the back. "Good job, *amigo*." Then he pointed to Lafourcade, Lihn, Miller Williams, Jodorowsky, and Stella. "So what's with them?"

"Miller says Chile needs educational reform and Alejandro says Chile needs more naked ladies," said Luis.

"Chile needs more than educational reform," replied Osvaldo. "Allesandri's policies are too timid. Reform in Chile will be deep and it will have to equal revolution."

"*Los momias* will never give us anything. Look at Bulnes. The rich bastard is stone-walling even reasonable demands," said Ramón Güarei.

Osvaldo nodded. "If Frei and the Christian Democrats win, the Radical Party will block their effort to dismantle the *fundos*. In the meantime, in the *callampas*—no clean water? No sanitation? The *obreros* will rise up. It will be *lucha armada*. Armed struggle for sure."

"It's the only way. *Lucha armada*. Look at Cuba," said Jesús.

From the other table, Stella blew a smoke ring at them. "I'm coming to join you *jovenes*," she said. "*Lucha armada*—I like that." Stella raised her fist. "*Muerte a los momias!*" Ramón, Osvaldo, and Jesús grinned.

The front door opened again, letting in another cold blast of air. Four people were silhouetted against the winter light. Their faces were in shadow, but Luis recognized Hector Körner Bulnes, Santiago del Campo, Odalís Luco Errázuriz, and his beloved Wefe, on their way toward them. Del Campo had a big grin. The laconic Hector was behind him; then Odalís, wearing a coat of heavy fur. Wefe, a confused Ophelia, in a fluffy rabbit-skin jacket, brought up the rear. Luis wished they hadn't come. Things had been tense between Osvaldo and Hector ever since the ill-fated cocktail party at Villavicencio.

Santiago slid onto the bench next to his former rival, Ramón. "*Qué pasa?*" Ramón gave him a cold look.

"We're talking about educational reform."

"With all Chile's problems, you should be talking *revolución, hombre*. Not *política*, but *pistolas!*" He clapped Ramón hard on the shoulder. Ramón winced.

Odalís had squeezed into a chair next to Stella. Hector helped to arrange her coat. It gleamed luxuriant and tawny next to Stella's mangy fur. Odalís's amber skin was glowing from the cold air outside.

"Actually, we *are* talking revolution," Stella said, "Marxist revolution, *amigos*."

Hector Körner Bulnes stared at her. "Chile doesn't need international Communism. *Chile ayuda a Chile.* Chile will help Chile."

"Well, your *mamá* has a big *fundo* in Parral. I hear it's over a thousand *hectares.* How much *ayuda* is she giving back to Chile? Or is this *ayuda* all for herself?"

Hector Körner Bulnes looked at her with an expression of distaste. "That land has been in our family for generations."

"And how many *inquilinos*—how many tenant farmers— work these ancestral lands of the Körner Bulnes?"

"The Bulnes take care of their own," said Hector.

"The Bulnes take care of themselves," corrected Stella. "Can her tenants even read the little papers your mother uses to settle her accounts? I hear she prints up the scrip herself. She doesn't pay her *inquilinos* in escudos."

"Stella!" Wefe interrupted. "You're being rude!"

Hector's pale mineral complexion was turning red. "Forget it, Wefe. We all know her. The *famous* poet Stella Diaz Varín. A Communist, like all the rest of them." Hector was spitting out the words. "The poets of Chile are all a bunch of Communists, and they're all published by Bolshevik presses—like those Arancibia Hermanos out in Independencia."

Stella leaned forward toward Hector. "Then will you write me a note of introduction to Agustín Edwards? Suggest he publish my latest poem? It's called *Porqué somos indecentes?* If *El Mercurio* would print it in their Sunday supplement, I'd forget about the Bolshevik presses."

Now Accursio's ears pricked up. "You have a problem with the Arancibia Hermanos, *hombre?*"

"They're behind this strike in Barrio Brasil. Everything they churn out is Marxist propaganda. They should stick to printing menus."

"Menus!" said Accursio, excitedly. "But that's my new book—*Menus de Lo Malo*. Do you think a Bolshevik press like Arancibia Brothers would print it?"

"Max Arancibia is a Communist lackey. Someone should shut him down." Hector's normally sullen skin had broken out in small red spots, as if iron oxides of the Atacama desert were all surfacing in his cheeks and forehead.

"Next my roommate will propose to burn all the books," said Santiago, cheerfully. "I'll have to have a talk with my vice-president."

Accursio had his hand over his mouth. His thoughts were twirling with Macchiavellian machinations. Stella Diaz Varín blew a smoke ring at him.

"And you, Accursio? So quiet?"

"Sorry—lost track of the conversation. Where were we?"

"The Bolshevik presses," said Santiago. He seemed in excellent humor. Odalís was glowing. Wefe was very quiet, Luis noticed. Osvaldo opened his guitar case and started singing in a low voice.

> *Minero soy,*
> *a la mina voy,*
> *a la muerte voy.*
> *Todo para que?*
> *Nada para mi.*

Osvaldo hummed the words under his breath, but Ramón and Jesús came in with loud voices on the chorus.

> *Todo para qué?*
> *Nada para mí!*

It was a crazy mix-up of a scene. Hector Körner Bulnes, with his pale, bony face. Stella, *la bandera*, smoking like a chimney. Santiago del Campo, the progressive student leader—not. Beautiful Odalís, she of the interesting mouth— where did she fit into this? Did she have something going with Hector? He had been so solicitous with the tawny fur. Wefe, in her fluffy little rabbit skin, looking a bit left out. Then his socialist pals, Osvaldo and Ramón and Jesús, so out of place, all of them, oblivious of disapproval, singing their hearts out. What a mad bedlam medley of a scene, everyone so mixed up.

> *No canto por cantar, ni por tener buena voz.*
> *Canto porque la guitarra tiene sentido y razon.*

Osvaldo was singing another Jara song under his breath.

"*Tú tienes buena voz, hombre,*" Stella said. She turned to Accursio. "Ask Osvaldo to read your poems for you next time, Accursio. At least he doesn't have guacamole mouth." Stella was being mean tonight, Luis thought. She could let any one of us have it.

Osvaldo set down his guitar. "I fear for my country. If Allende gets elected, the right will take violent action. And if Allende doesn't win, the people will rise up. Either way I see *una lucha armada.*"

Hector's lips were pressed together to the point they were almost invisible—a thin white cut at the bottom of his face. He was clenching and unclenching his fists. Osvaldo placed his battered cap on his head, picked up his guitar case, and made for the door, followed by Ramón and Jesús.

"*Venceremos!*" shouted Ramón, pumping his fist in the air.

"*Poder a lo pueblo!*" shouted his friend.

"You're so sure revolution is inevitable?" Santiago called out after them. There was no answer but the sound of the door closing on the back of Osvaldo's trademark shabby grey jacket.

So why had Señor Sonrisa been in such a good mood at El Bosco? Wefe reported that the Presidente de los Estudiantes had recently given an important speech. The theme? That Chileans had to disavow the *ultras*, the extreme elements of both parties. On the left Santiago had pointed to the Socialist priest, Antonio Zamorano, as a naïve populist who knew nothing of governing and who would turn Chile into a Marxist state. He also pointed to the Catalan Stalinists, the Hermanos Arancibia, who were stirring up class warfare with pamphlets like this forthcoming *Sangrientas Luchas de los Obreros Chilenos*. On the right the student president had summoned up the visage of General Abdón Barrientos whose *mano dura* was so rude, so uncivilized, so very un-Chilean. The general disgraced Chile internationally. He totally lacked social skills. His values and beliefs represented a throwback to a strongman era and did not represent Chile of the 20th century.

Hector's father (who was Santiago's godfather) had arranged for the handsome student leader to give this speech at the Club Unión. Students were also invited, at least those who had paid their FeCH dues. This limited the number considerably. So how had it gone?

There had been some problems. Many members of the Club Unión were conservative in their views and viewed the *mano dura* candidate, General Barrientos, with enthusiasm. And some of the FeCH students felt Allende was a compromiser. Many of them had campaigned for the Socialist priest. Nonetheless Del Campo had spoken well—clearly, confidently—with an articulate message. To Allende's *vía pacífica,* Del Campo—and here his eyebrows formed their charming, quizzical triangle—dare he set his *vía de la mitad?* His way was positioned exactly halfway between two extremes. His father had been satisfied. It was clear Santiago's political career was bright.

But Hector Körner Bulnes had cooled on Santiago a little after the presentation. Hector's father, the godfather Santiago Körner, had sat with the group who preferred Barrientos. Hector himself favored a military solution because of the need for standards, and discipline. Both Hector and his father held sacred the memory of Emil Körner, the German forebear who had came to stiffen the spine of the Chilean army.

Now Wefe said something interesting. The big reason why Santiago had begged his godfather to set up the Club Unión speech had to do with him, Luis. Santiago had paid attention when Luis brought down the house with his jazzed-up poetry reading. He had seen the tender kiss Wefe bestowed upon her former lover. He had even noted the (to him, undue) amount of attention Accursio Chiarello got with his Llu-llooo-jacko poems. Santiago felt competitive. Why should *estranjeros*—a *gringo* and a *porteño*—be camped out in the limelight when he, Santiago, was a so much more gifted orator—and with a hell of a lot more to say?

So the whole Club Unión thing was just payback to Luis. To establish once and for all who was cock of the roost.

The second Sunday of August. Tito Bustos and Chico Silva look out of place in the apartment on Villavicencio. Tito's ox frame is splayed out on a white leather armchair, his belly protruding Jello-like over his belt buckle. His dirty fist is pressed into his cheek; he is frowning.

Chico—slight, furtive, evasive—leans against the wall, sucking nervously on a cigarette. The only guest who is totally at ease is Accursio Chiarello, whose elongated body is draped on the white leather sofa. His feet in handsome Argentine boots rest on the glass coffee table.

Hector Körner Bulnes stands before an easel on which he has propped a large pad of paper. Tacked to the wall

61

behind him is a 6-foot by 4-foot Chilean flag—a single red band at the bottom, a blue square on the upper left enclosing a five-pointed white star. *La Estrella Solutaria*—the national flag of Chile resembles a cruelly truncated Stars and Stripes. Under the flag he has pinned a map of Santiago, with a large red X at the intersection of Avenidas Coronel Alvarado and Luis Galdames. Hector's normally bone-white face shows a flush of pink on the cheekbones.

"Gentlemen," he says. "To be successful, three things are needed. The know-how. The raw materials. And the opportunity to present our little gift." On the word "gift," Hector minces his lips. You might say the know-how, the when, and the where." Then he grows serious. "Gentleman. I have the know-how."

Carefully Hector draws a large circle, then draws a second circle a quarter inch inside the first. "This is the bomb casing, gentleman," he says. "We will use this fisherman's float." He kicks a basketball-sized metal sphere at his feet. From the sound, it is clear the sphere is hollow. The bomb-to-be rolls a short distance and stops at the edge of the carpet.

Hector draws cross-hatchings inside his circle. "This, gentlemen, is the explosive powder. It is sodium nitrate, mined here in our beloved *patria,* mined in our own Atacama desert, converted to ammonium nitrate, and mixed with trinitrotoluene."

"TNT," grunts Tito. He knows about this stuff.

"Correct. TNT mixed with ammonium nitrate is Amatol."

"Amatol! I love it!" cries Accursio. "I love it all!"

Hector draws a narrow rectangle inside the sphere, extending almost to the middle. Moistening his lips, he carefully pens a tiny clock face within the rectangle. At the top he draws a single wiggly line extending out. "And this, gentleman, is the blasting cap and arming device."

"*Guapo!*" cries Chico. His face is shining. To be in on something big like this.

Accursio's grin is stretching from ear to ear. He's beginning to feel the bomb in his bones, the bomb in his belly. It's his baby, his only begotten son.

"*Bonita bomba!*" he exclaims.

"My own invention," says Hector. The entire design comes from a military textbook, but why shouldn't Hector take credit?

The three guests examine the drawing with various expressions: Accursio, smiling from silly and secretive pleasure; Tito, grunting appreciatively; and Chico giggling from nervous euphoria.

Hector basks for a minute or two in their approval, but then he straightens his frame. "So, gentlemen, who will get the *nitro*?"

"I can get the powder," says Tito. "There's a bucket at Barrio Brasil. It's locked up, but I have the key." He gives the others a knowing wink, a big squint of his left eyelid.

Chico squashes his cigarette between his thumb and forefinger and flips the butt toward the crystal ashtray on the coffee table. The butt ricochets off Accursio's shiny boot and lands on the floor.

"Careful, man," grumbles Accursio. Taking an ironed handkerchief, he flicks off an invisible residue of ash from his boot.

Hector looks at his guests sternly. "Gentleman. The final step. We've agreed on the where, but we need the when and the who."

"I'll be the who," says Accursio. "If anyone asks, I'm showing Arancibia the manuscript of my *Menus de lo Malo*."

"The *bomba* will be set to go off 60 seconds after you light the fuse," said Hector. "You'll need to move fast. And you'll need a look-out, someone who will make sure the coast is clear."

"I'll go with him," says Chico. His dark, furtive face is glistening with anticipation. "I used to be a *carabinero*."

"You *were* a *carabinero?*" says Hector. "Not now? What happened?"

"They kicked me out."

Hector frowns. A failed *carabinero?* He has hoped for much better. He has hoped the team would be a credit to great-grandfather Emil. But the plan is unfolding.

"Accursio, with Chico, agreed?" asks Hector. There are grunts, and nods. "And the when, gentlemen?"

"Thursday of the *Fiestas Patrias*," says Accursio. "Arancibia will be printing *Sangrientas Luchas de los Obreros Chilenos*."

"Using our sacred patriotic holiday to print Bolshevik garbage?" Hector's jaw trembles in a savage grimace. Then he claps his hands. "So be it. Gentlemen. Thursday of *Fiestas Patrias*. Accursio, with Chico. Plan to be here at noon. The little gift will be ready."

Accursio nods. His Macchiavellian genes are vibrating. His scheme to manipulate these right-wing idiots is succeeding beyond his wildest hopes. When the Taller Gráfico blows up, García's *Calculated Lion* will be nothing more than a pile of ashes.

Tito has been chewing his thumb. "What's the code? We gotta have a code."

"We need a *contraseña,*" chimes in Chico.

Hector looks blank.

"Remember PUMA?" growls Tito. "Seven years ago."

Hector brightens. "Ah, yes. PUMA. *Por una mañana auspiciosa.* My uncles were part of that." In the mid-fifties a military group plotted to overthrow the Ibañez presidency.

They called themselves *la linea recta,* the straight path, and their code was PUMA. For an auspicious tomorrow.

"How about *mali?*" suggests Accursio. *"Muerte a la izquierda.* Death to the left."

"How about *gali?*" offers Tito. *"Golpe a la izquierda.* Blow to the left."

"I want *dali,*" says Chico, so happy to be part of this. *"Daño a la izquierda.* Harm to the left."

"Okay, gentlemen," says Hector. *"Maligalidali."*

"Too many syllables," objects Accursio. "No more than four. Please. Can we chop off the *dali?*""

"You're proposing *maligali?*" Hector stares at the Argentine. Accursio shrugs.

"Too short," growls Tito. "Look. We had it right the first time."

"Maligalidali," says Chico. It is always good to agree with the boss.

Hector feels frustrated, but he has to work with what he's got. "Okay. Everyone? *Maligalidali.* Let's stand and pledge allegiance to the *patria.* Right hands on your hearts, my friends, and raise your left arm to the Chilean flag."

Tito stumbles to his feet; Chico is already standing. Accursio unfolds himself. "I can't salute," he says.

"Why not?"

"I'm Argentine."

"Are you in, or are you out?

"I'm in, man."

'So do it," orders Hector. *"Maligalidali!"*

Maligalidali repeats the group in unison.

Four hands on four hearts. Three arms stretched high to honor the Chilean flag. A fourth arm is raised but barely to half-mast, and slithers down without straightening its elbow.

Hector is satisfied.

Maligalidali. The plan is set.

The three conspirators stumble out, and Hector is unpinning the enormous Chilean flag from the wall when a noise startles him. It is Wefe, emerging from Santiago's bedroom. She is sleepy, half-drunk, wearing only a T-shirt. Hector can't take his eyes off her bare legs. She looks vacant, lost, scared.

Her eyes move toward the map of Santiago with its big red X, bright and uneven as melted red candle wax, over the words Arancibia Hermanos. Hector follows her gaze. On the easel is the diagram of the bomb. He jumps and starts turning the drawings over rapidly, but she's seen plenty.

August eleventh was Stella's birthday. How old was she? Luis did not know. Sometimes she said thirty-five, but other times thirty-seven. Or was it thirty-nine? Which was it? She would shrug. "Does it make any difference?"

He spent most evenings in her company, at El Bosco, or the Café Iris, or La Casa de las Botellas, or at her house out in Maipu, rolling reefers and listening to jazz LPs. Dexedrine was available at pharmacies without a prescription and they often stayed up all night. She had an Zenith portable stereo— the Deluxe Model. The speakers disconnected from the box and were placed around the room. The Deluxe Model's sound quality was terrible, but a toke of dope helped. One could make out the clear, pure notes of Art Pepper or Charlie Mingus through the buzz.

They sat on the floor beside a low table which held a sputtering candle and cups of cold tea. Books were stacked in piles along the walls. Luis tried to ignore the strong odor of cat piss, which was not masked by the sweet Indian incense Stella burned. He and Stella were smoking some Ecuadorian bud using a new water-pipe, a birthday present from Luis.

Hit, smoke, hit, smoke, hit, smoke, bass line curves, arches up, candle flame sputters.

"Shit, man. This music is so cool! Not like that *folclórico* music that your friend Osvaldo thinks is so great!" Stella was leaning back, her eyes closed. She had put her bare feet up on Luis's lap. Her voice was smoky and fun.

Luis reflected there was no good Spanish word for "fun." You could say, "I enjoyed myself," or "I disfruted myself," but simple *fun*? *Diversión* with its connotations of a detour, or *alegría,* with its elements of uni-dimensional marching-band major-keys, didn't make it. Nor did *placer* capture the effervescence, the pure bubbliness, of fun. He moved, and the bare feet of Stella flopped onto the floor. There could be a little too much *fun* around the smoky-voiced one. He had to be careful when she started with her long drawn-out "Luisito's."

He studied her face. It was a strong face. There was no extra flesh on it, and her mouth was so reddish-pink, a mashed strawberry. They were not lovers, but she was always trying to get him into bed.

Why did he resist?

He was twenty-four, she was thirty-five—or was it thirty-seven?—in any case the difference alarmed him. She knew too much. About herself. About him. About life. She would have too much power. She was his *compa*, his trusted *amiga,* his friend. He had absolutely no plans to go to bed with her. Anyway he was still in love with Wefe.

The phone was ringing.

A rumble in the hallway, heavy footsteps. Tito Bustos was home. His voice was booming as it always did. He always shouted. He spent the day shouting at workers in Barrio Brasil, shouting up at them as they dangled from scaffolding and beams. He shouted that they didn't know anything, didn't know how to do anything, didn't listen to him. Since the short-lived *huelga*, he had been booming more than ever. He had sided with Bulnes, and his men didn't trust him. He was shouting now.

The fucking powder? *El coño nitro?* Chico will take care of it. Chico will get it. *No te preocupe! Vos! Sí! Sí! Sí! Sí! Sí! Maligalidali, sí!* A sound of a receiver being slammed back into its cradle.

"Oh, he's back," Stella said. She stared at her water pipe, then arose and placed it in a cupboard. "He'll come in and smell the dope," she said. "Let's get out of here." They exited through a back door that led to an weedy patch of a garden, then out a rusted gate to an alley. In the cold air, Stella laughed. "That *coño*," she said. "I swear I'm going to leave him."

She put her arm through Luis's. "I'm flat broke. That bastard doesn't give me a cent. Lend me a few *lucas?*" Loans to Stella were never repaid. But she was his friend. It was her birthday. And the Mertins Foundation was generous.

"*Si?*" Stella said. She threw her arm over his shoulder, pulling him against her. There was always this push-pull around Stella. He was both attracted and put off. He still loved Wefe, his slender Ophelia, her long, pale hair, her delicate bones. Wefe was a beautiful *fleur-du-lys*, his lily girl, and Stella was a flamboyant orange canna. A big girl, too, with heavy bones and solid flesh, an ox woman. Too big a girl for him. Yet Luis was a man and a sexual being. Stella's invitations were at times of considerable interest.

Yes, and thinking about it, he was also sick of Accursio's calling him Pen-Rod. What—had the Argentine been forced to read Booth Tarkington in some English class? Pen-Rod. He gets it. It's phallic—in Accursio's mind. It's Accursio's way of calling him, Luis, a prick, and Luis is sick of it. He is going to have to deal with this Pen-Rod shit. And yet for the moment he doesn't act on any of this, this Hamlet of a Luis.

Soon Luis and Stella are chatting and laughing boisterously at La Casa de las Botellas, making fun of the two Enriques or the pathetic little Eliana Navarro. Mother of God. They laugh until they are sobbing.

They are cruel, and sometimes being cruel is fun.

Chapter Four

Luis and Stella are at her place, listening to Dexter Gordon on the Deluxe Model. They will head over to El Bosco later where Accursio will be reading, but in the meantime they are discussing the little cards which have arrived from Pablo Neruda.

On one side Neruda has drawn two primitive figures, a man and a woman, waving white handkerchiefs over their heads, with the hand-lettered words, *Baila Septiembre baila, con los pies de la patria,* printed at the bottom with Neruda's signature. On the other side is an invitation to a party on 18 September 1963. The *Fiestas Patrias* celebrate Chile's independence from Spain, and Neruda invites all his friends to enjoy the magnificent view of the fireworks over Valparaiso Bay from his house, La Sebastiana. His wide circle includes Chile's left-wing writers, artists, politicians, and diplomats. Luis is honored to have received a little card. Maybe Parra has given his name to Don Pablo.

The Calculated Lion is scheduled to be printed the following day and Luis plans to witness the birth of his book. *Las Sangrientas Luchas de los Obreros Chilenos* will be printed in the morning. Luis should be there shortly after twelve, when *The Calculated Lion* will roll off the press. They can take a bus to Valparaiso Wednesday afternoon, attend Neruda's party that evening, and crash that night with a friend of Stella's, Gastón Flores Rubio, who runs a rooming house on Cerro Concepción. Then the next morning they will return to Santiago and taxi out to Avenida Coronel Alvarado.

A banging door, then heavy footsteps. Stella's husband is home. Through the open doorway they see Tito Bustos standing in the drafty hallway in his dirty plaid jacket. His uncombed hair sticks out around his head. The telephone is ringing. Bustos presses the Bakelite receiver to his ear.

"*Maligalidali.*"

That is weird.

"*El nitro? Listo,*" growls Tito. He slams the receiver down and scratches his cheek with a dirty forefinger. Then he takes a folded piece of paper out of his pocket and studies it, frowning.

"What the fuck is all the baby-talk about?" yells Stella."

"None of your business."

"Were you talking to Chico Silva?"

"What the hell business is it of yours?"

"That *coño* is a fucking Fascist."

"He's a *varón*. He has *cojones*. What do poets do in a fight? Throw flowers at each other?" Tito makes a little mincing gait, his voice high-pitched. "Take that!" he lisps.

Stella moves to the doorway. "Stop it, Tito, or I'll show you who's got the *cojones* here."

"Oh, yeah, I forgot—you're the *boxerena.* Well, there's only one man in this house, and it ain't you." He slaps her hard but Stella is so solid, the blow hardly touches her. "You keep your nose out of my business." Tito slaps her again.

Stella slams her fist into her husband's face, knocking him against the wall. He crumples to the floor. Tito's head lies at a strange angle, blood trickling out of his nose. Then Tito is stroking his nose with his hand, holding it up to look at the blood on it.

She grabs her mangy fur coat and pushes Luis out the back door. "Let's get out of here."

The fresh air is welcome after the heavy Indian incense and the cat's piss, and the domestic commotion. Luis is glad to get away.

"Why do you stay with him?" Luis asks.

"Big *pijo*," says Stella.

At El Bosco they found Accursio sitting on a stool at the side of the stage. He was wearing a large cloak. His boot heels were hooked on a rung of the stool so that his folded knees were only inches from his nose. He held a long scroll of white paper.

The reading had been called without much notice. There were few people in the room. The two Enriques had come; the mousy Christian poet, Eliana Navarro, Armando Menedín; a few others. Jodorowsky had returned to Paris.

Eliana Navarro was gazing at Accursio with an expression that made Stella snort. She inhaled her cigarette, before coughing. "Looks like she's eaten too much of the Fatal Empanada."

Armando was master of ceremonies. "Ladies and gentlemen," he declaimed, "It is my pleasure to bring you a poet you've all heard so much about, a young man who, having made a big splash in his own country—"

"—a splash straight into the Rio Plata," whispered Stella, "and if we're lucky, he'll drown!"

"—a big splash in Buenos Aires, a big splash in Ar-hen-teena," Armando continued,

"—enough splashing, man," said Stella. "I'm getting wet."

"—a poet not yet thirty, whose poems have appeared in some of the best magazines—"

"—like *Epimetheus*?" Stella raised her eyebrows.

"—a poet who has inaugurated an entirely new genre within poetry—*cocinismo*—or *food poetry!*" declaimed Armando.

"I'm sick already," said Stella, sticking her finger in her mouth. "It must be *food poetry* poisoning."

"From the grand, great city of Buenos Aires—"

"Putas Aires," whispered Stella,

"The one and the only—Accursio Chiarello!"

There was a patter of applause. Accursio unfolded himself and stood up. He looked pleased, although he had been greeted by nothing but the scraping of chairs, the rustling of papers, the coughing and clearing of throats.

"*La Bomba!*" he shouted.

The poem began with a reference to *la bomba* as a pastry filled with whipped cream, candied orange peel, and little chunks of bittersweet chocolate. But then *la bomba* morphed into an irresistible woman (Argentine, presumably) whose long hair hung down to her ass, a woman who possessed the key to a great secret which the poet both wished and did not wish to reveal. Suddenly Accursio was at the climax of his poem and the figure of the woman had given way to images of menace. Accursio was shrieking, like a huge strange bird in his dark cloak, that

> *La bomba is coming,*
> *La bomba is here,*
> *La bomba will equalize,*
> *La bomba will penalize,*
> *La bomba will open doors*
> *La bomba will close them,*
> *Let us welcome, welcome, welcome*
> *la bomba.*

Accursio stood under the spotlight, screeching. Sweat poured down his forehead. He drew the back of his left hand across his brow and slowly set scroll of paper down on the stool. He gazed out at the audience as if he were in a trance.

The small audience, too, seemed tranced. It took those present several minutes to respond, to digest what they had just heard. Then there was more rustling, coughing, throat-clearing, scraping of chairs.

Only Armando Menedín had the presence of mind to leap up to the stage, his rotund little figure bustling with energy. "Bravo, bravo!" he cried, clapping both plump palms. "Bravíssimo!"

Armando turned to the audience with an ornate flourish of the arm, a sweeping gesture which ended with his open palm pointing directly to Accursio. "A tour de force, ladies and gentlemen, Superb. Spectacular. *Extraordinario!*"

Armando was clapping and clapping and clapping, and this roused the audience from its narcoleptic silence. A few palms came together, then a few more, fitfully, until finally everyone in the room was clapping, then standing, then shouting "Bravo!" in brave, strong voices; although, as Luis glanced around him, those standing seemed gripped in a narcotic trance—clapping and crying, yes, but with vacant faces, vacant eyes. It was as if some powerful *brujo* had filled their wine-glasses with *lethe,* the drink of forgetting.

Accursio stepped down from the stage. Luis knew he must acknowledge his friend's triumph—if that's what it was. Luis went forward. "Far out, man. Formidable. Not sure I quite got it, but good show." Luis was stumbling. He didn't get it. But it took *cojones* to try something new. Luis should know. Accursio stared at him as if he did not see him. Stella tugged at Luis's coat sleeve.

"I think he's high," she whispered. "Let's go."

Then Accursio's eyes opened. For one long second, his eyes bore into Luis in a venomous stare. "It's for you, Pen-Rod," he hissed.

That was all he said.

As they left, Luis was startled to see Tito Bustos enter El Bosco. He had wadded white tissue paper into one of his nostrils. His gait was slack, yet the man seemed hyper-alert.

The skinny-assed Chico Silva was with him, talking intently to Accursio.

Stella and Luis hurried out into the night.

"What was Tito doing there?" Luis asked her, after a few cold, rainy blocks. "He's never been keen on poetry."

"Was he there? I didn't see him. Don't worry about him. Let's go get a drink." And they hurried down the dark, damp blocks of Santiago to the welcoming lights of the Casa de las Botellas.

The bus arrived in Valparaiso late Wednesday afternoon. Stella and Luis began the long climb from the bus station up Cerro Bellavista. Stella was wearing a tight green skirt which outlined her haunches, a rose silk blouse with plunging décolletage, a bright yellow scarf. As they puffed and panted up Yerbas Buenas, and Avenida Alemania, then Calle Ferrari, men leered at her with low sucking sounds and whistles. The driver of a delivery truck leaned out his window and moved his tongue rapidly over his lips. A little newsboy at the corner of Ferrari and Alemania was the only innocent, calling the evening paper in a haunting clear solo line, "*La Tra-a-a-a-y-oh!*"

Pablo Neruda awaited his guests at the door of La Sebastiana. His Indian face, with its full cheeks and heavy-lidded eyes, was lit up with pleasure. He was forming a double chin. He wore pleated trousers, a loose shirt; his belly was prominent.

"Welcome, welcome!" he said to them. At his side, *la chascona*, she of the wild locks, had tamed them into a prim Duchess of Windsor roll. She wore a high-necked blouse and a black skirt.

Don Pablo kissed Stella effusively on both cheeks. His heavy-lidded eyes gazed straight down her cleavage. Matilde looked away with the slightest frown of annoyance before turning back brightly. She pointed them toward a wrought iron spiral staircase, almost pushing them up it. Behind them a new wave of guests crowded, waiting to be greeted.

The spiral stairs led to a patio with a view. Valparaiso was a low city, built on hills, with fantastic white ocean light like San Francisco. In the bay were anchored the big warships of the Chilean naval fleet; smaller boats further out in the water would launch the fireworks later. Nearer, along the waterfront, was the bustle of Chile's great port. Horses pulled heavy wagons. Mules with sacks, and *huasos* on horseback, wearing flat black caps, shared the road with buses, cars, trucks and trolleys.

The wind smelled of fish and salt water and blew Stella's red hair back from her face. She looked like a ship's figurehead, Luis thought. *La bandera.* This striking woman was the friend, the confidante, most likely the lover (at one time or another) of most of the men at this gathering. He was proud to be seen with her.

A waiter in a short white coat hustled by, holding a tray high above his head. Luis accepted a whiskey and stared out at the bay. To be here, at Neruda's most famous party, with his book going to press the next day . . . was it not all happening? Now?

"To *me!*" he breathed. A silent, but heartfelt, toast.

Many guests were gathered on the patio now. Enrique Lihn and Enrique Lafourcade stood by the rail, facing someone Luis did not recognize. The stranger was sitting on a stone bench covered with cushions. He leaned back into pillows, his right ankle resting on his left knee. A beefy hand, thick-fingered, grasped a glass of red wine. He wore a white suit and square-framed black eyeglasses. Luis noted the thick cheeks, not yet jowls, the incipient double chin.

Stella jumped. "Oh, my God, it's Allende!"

77

Enrique Lihn was taking a seat next to the candidate. Their bulks were somewhat equal. "So, Señor Candidate," said Lihn expansively. "What exactly is your platform?

"*Empanadas y vino tinto—para todos!*" Allende and Lihn clinked glasses. The bevy surrounding them tittered appreciatively.

"Foreign capital is plundering Chile," said Lihn.

"You're right," said the candidate. "The fate of Chile is negotiated in the Club de Paris. So what do I propose? The biggest reform—we nationalize the copper mines. Those profits flowing to the United States must flow back to the *patria*. We break up the *fundos* and eliminate Chile's dependence on American wheat and corn."

A hubbub of voices followed.

"Don't be surprised to see American fingerprints all over the upcoming election," said Lihn.

"If there are fingerprints, you won't see them," responded Allende. "The question is, will Kennedy respect Chile's right to self-government? Cold War pressure in America could force him to act against us."

"Will the CIA respect Chile's right to self-government? That's the question," said Lihn. "There's Kennedy's policy. And then there's the real *policy*."

"Do you want to meet him?" whispered Stella.

"Maybe later," said Luis. He felt unprepared to talk Chilean politics. He would only embarrass himself.

Stella shrugged.

"Ah, *la bandera!*" Allende had seen her and rose to his feet, with a big smile.

Luis found himself in a large room lined with antique maps. Mermaids lifted wet tresses from archaic seas; monsters disported themselves at the four points of the compass. The renderings of the European and American continents were misshapen. Through windows which resembled port holes, the hills of Valapariso were visible, with a hazy milky-blue sky over all. Everyone was there. Hector Körner Bulnes. Santiago Del Campo. Odalís Luco Errázuriz. Santiago Del Campo's head was inclined, listening to his cousin. Although she had been schooled by nuns, something in the tremble of her mouth suggested a woman who could be extremely passionate, Luis thought.

Luis made his way toward Nicanor Parra. He was talking to a woman who looked familiar. Where had he seen her before?

"I want you to meet Danielle Allende," said Parra. The woman was staring hard at him. She had thick, dark unruly hair. Then Luis remembered. On the airplane. The woman in the pink dress. She who smelled of violets.

"The poet from Berkeley! So you *have* come to see my beautiful Valparaiso!" She kissed him on one cheek and then the other, as if they were old friends. Her body was soft.

"Guess what? I will be in your Berkeley next month! I've been accepted into the graduate program in landscape design." Her eyes flashed a bold glance, but she pouted, "I know no one there. I will be terribly lonely."

"When I return in December, I can show you around," said Luis. The party was in full buzz. Fred Langhorst was talking to the Italian ambassador. Wefe stood by her father's side in a white dress, her hair streaming down her back. Even mousy Eliana Navarro was there with an unexpected husband—older than she, distinguished looking. Luis saw Accursio Chiarello chatting with them. Plump little Armando Menedín made his way over to Luis, giving a thumbs-up. "Tomorrow! You'll be a published author."

Neruda's big belly was pressed against the bar's pewter counter. *"Coquetelón, Don Luis?"* he said. Happily he surveyed an array of Portuguese wine glasses. Emerald green, garnet red, amethyst, topaz. "Wine tastes better when drunk from colored glasses!" His laugh filled the room.

Neruda poured cognac, champagne, Cointreau, orange juice into a cobalt blue glass and handed it to Luis. The *coquetelón* was Neruda's specialty and it was very light on the orange juice. Stella was holding an emerald green glass, standing so close to Luis that he could barely raise his glass without bumping his arm into her décolletage. "Salud!" She clinked glasses with Don Pablo, then with Luis, then with the Italian ambassador who was now standing close by.

"*A la patria!*" said Don Pablo.

"*A la vida!*" Stella downed the *coqueletón* in one gulp.

At another point Luis found himself in the bathroom doing lines with Accursio and Señor Sonrisa. The floor swam in patterns of green, blue and white tiles. The heels of their shoes made tapping sounds on the tiles. They laughed and jostled each other, passing a rolled *escudo* note back and forth. Luis caught their reflection in the enormous gilt-framed mirror . . . three impossibly handsome young men, arrogant, confident, cocky, entitled. Their heels clacking on the floor reminded Luis of three flamenco dancers—arrogant, haughty. High.

Accursio had unfolded himself, standing even taller than usual. He could have been a *caballero* out of a Goya painting. Señor Sonrisa's white teeth gleamed in his chiseled face. But tonight—perhaps it was the coke—Luis was not irritated by Del Campo's insolent manner. The guy was interesting. Perhaps he had something to offer. Armed revolutionary struggle—well, why not? No, wait—that was Osvaldo Güareí. Santiago was going to work within the system. Whatever.

Accursio? A great guy. A talented character, doing very interesting things with his *food poetry*. What's not to like? thought Luis, expansively. It took *cojones* to read that bomb poem. What a blast that had been. The guy had balls. He had talent.

Certainly everyone was getting on like a house afire. Who had produced the white powder? Accursio? Or was it Del Campo? Later Stella said it had probably been Don Pablo himself. Neruda was very open-minded. He wanted his young guests to have a good time.

He, Luis, was feeling like the cock of the walk. He was almost strutting. He was at the best party, with the best people, with the most stunning woman at this gathering. Stella Diaz Varín. And tomorrow he would be a published author, his book of poems printed by the famous Arancibia Hermanos. It didn't get better than this.

Wefe Langhorst was present, but she seemed inexplicably different. She looked pale, unadorned; in a room of brilliant women flaunting their sexuality, she was plain. Her body was too slender. Her long pale hair struck Luis as colorless; her white dress, flat shoes, uncertain demeanor, made Luis impatient. He noted Señor Sonrisa spending a lot of time tonight talking to his beautiful cousin.

Wefe seemed to be trying to get Luis's attention. More than once he had had to shrug off those cold little fingers grabbing at his arm. "Luis! We've got to talk."

After all those nights knocking on your door? And it was always, no, I'm tired, I'm busy, please go away? No, not tonight, he thought, my best night—but she had finally cornered him on the staircase. He was stumbling down to the patio to listen to Allende's conversation and also to establish a good view of the fireworks to come. He was going down; she was coming up. She put her fingers into his belt.

"We need to talk."

"It can wait."

"It can't wait."

"I'll catch you later."

"No! Hector—Accursio—" but Luis pushed past her. Her pleading face was so waif-like, so Ophelia-like. Well, tonight was his Hamlet night—if all the world's a stage, tonight he was a *big* player. No longer in the middle of a dark woods, he had emerged into the light. The limelight. And it was fantastic.

By eight the sun had gone down, leaving cloudy streaks of crimson, rose, violet on the horizon. Neruda told a story about Lautaro, the Mapuche hero who had led the assault against the Spanish *conquistadores*. Lautaro killed General Don Valdiviana by forcing him to drink a cup of molten gold.

Neruda waved his arm. Maybe Don Valdiviana had been forced to drink the sunset itself! And Don Pablo filled more Portuguese glasses, saying the molten gold served at La Sebastiana would send everyone straight to heaven. Then he disappeared, returning with a lacquer tray of marijuana cigarettes and a Chinese celadon bowl of morphine tablets. He winked and said he hoped everyone would have *fun*. He used the English word.

By nine o'clock the night had turned cold. Guests stood outside on the patio waiting for the fireworks. Allende was surrounded by his little group. Luis thought the presidential candidate looked tired.

From the black water of the harbor, eight crooked arms of light inched up into the sky. Their glowing verticals appeared at the periphery of Lu's vision, then they streaked up to collide front and center of the sky, bursting into fiery flowers which slowly fell apart. Then a second set of crooked lines snaked upward from the water, becoming round balls which exploded into red, orange, yellow, green fragments. The explosion was reflected on the bay as a spreading red glare with sliding white shards.

Everyone on the patio shouted.

There were explosions stacked on explosions. Five

seconds of darkness were followed by then another jagged white streak, inching skyward, erupting into a ruby circlet, with a square pendant of purple sparks. Then a second white streak would inch up to form a necklace of white diamonds with two pendants—one of emeralds, one of blue sapphires. A third white streak, then a third necklace—a circlet of many-colored brilliant drops and three pendants. It was a cloud of exploding Christmas ornaments. What was this fascination with *fuegos artificiales?* Would the sky look so different if real missiles were exploding overhead? Were humans hopelessly fascinated with the thrill of the dangerous, the noise and smell of war? An enormous spiky dahlia now exploded directly overhead, its colors changing from peach to green to red to white in intense 3-D. The guests were craning their necks and screaming. The sparks flared and then slowly disintegrated and vanished into the darkness of the sky, while from the water below four more snakes of light inched upward and met in the center of the heavens. They exploded into a glowing crimson rectangle, topped by a white rectangle, a blue square, opposite it, and in the center of the blue square, a five-pointed white star.

The guests on the patio screamed, whistled and clapped as they recognized the Chilean flag, a huge sky-sized billboard in the black night. In the glow of the explosions, their faces were chalky, their arms held high above their heads, palms clapping madly. All around Luis, Chileans were sobbing, delirious with nationalism. Then it was over. Pink smoke rose from the fire ships and an acrid gunpowder smell wafted over the rooftops of Valparaiso toward La Sebastiana.

Stella's breasts were pressed against his arm; then she moved so that her back was to him, her ass pressed up against his hips; and his arms were around her as they both faced seaward.

"I'm soooo cold, Luis," she shivered. "Warm me up." Coke or Cointreau or cognac or champagne . . . something had changed the rules tonight. He was no longer on guard with her. He no longer cared what anyone thought. Least of all, Wefe.

Luis woke up to the sound of pipes and tabors beating a simple rhythm outside the window. Simple, innocent piping. Some tenth-century French tune. Where was he? He felt Stella beside him on the sagging mattress. She was lying on her back, snoring, slightly. In the morning light her skin didn't look so creamy. It looked old. She looked old. Her mouth, slightly open as she snored, was no longer a bruised strawberry. It was a dried apricot with smeared lipstick.

Where were they? Ah, yes. Her friend, the painter, Gastón. The little alley of Pierre Loti, with the music school next door. Luis's head hurt. He shook Stella awake. "We've got to get back to Santiago."

"Why, Luisito?" she murmured.

"They're printing my book today."

"So?"

"So I want to watch Max print the run."

"You're loco, Luis. You think Max needs you?"

"It's important to me. You promised."

"Come here, Luisito." But Luisito was jumping out of bed and into his clothes.

At that very minute, in Washington, DC, Augustín Edwards' black Cadillac is gliding toward the White House. The owner of *El Mercurio* sits next to his bodyguard in the back seat. His long thin fingers grasp the ivory knob of a walking stick. The fingers are as pale as the ivory knob, their nails covered with a clear nail polish.

"Mr. President," he begins. "Salvador Allende could win the Presidency next year. There are many in my country who would find this extension of Marxism into Chile intolerable, Mr. President."

At one o'clock Stella and Luis are at the door of Avenida Coronel Alvarado 2602. The old Mergenthaler Linotyper can be heard clanking away inside the building. Luis rings the bell and Max Arancibia answers, wiping his fingers on his printer's apron. His near-set Catalan eyes open wider, seeing Luis.

"I didn't expect to see you today! Don Pablo's parties; I was sure you would not return. I was able to run off *Sangrientas Luchas* yesterday, and this morning I printed your book. But come in, come in—let me show you a copy," and as Max motions them in with his arm, Luis, from the corner of his eye, sees a figure round the corner to his right.

The figure—or figures, because suddenly there are two of them—are moving quickly.

It is Accursio Chiarello. Behind him is Chico Silva.

"Wha-a-a-a-t?" thinks Luis. Accursio? And Chico Silva—Tito's pal? Accursio is carrying a round object against his chest. It looks like a black bowling ball.

"Hey, man, what's up?" said Luis.

"Here's what's *up!*" shouts Accursio. He is raising his arms to hurl the thing.

"This is for you, Pen-Rod!" he screams with a mad grimace.

For Luis, the entire scene plays out in slow motion. He watches Accursio without being able to move. Max Arancibia peers from his door, open-mouthed. Fortunately Stella is operating in real time. The *boxerena* swings her arm. The object flies out of Accursio's arms and bounces down the cobblestones of Avenida Coronel Alvarado, coming to a stop at its intersection with Avenida Luis Galdames.

At that moment the limousine of General Abdón Barrientos rolls around the corner of Galdames and forward onto Avenida Coronel Alvarado. The General has just left a poker game at the home of his mistress, Piedad, a woman of the people.

The object lies directly in the path of the limousine.

"Run! Run! Run!" screams Stella. She grabs Luis's hand and drags him after her.

The last Luis sees of Accursio is his black pigtail streaming out behind his head, as he and Chico Silva disappear around the opposite corner. Something falls from the Argentine's jacket pocket, a small red book which lands in the gutter, but Luis barely registers this. Stella's powerful body is pulling him so hard his feet are off the ground as she yanks him toward the safety of Boulevard Las Araucarias.

KA BAM!

The sound of the explosion echoes and re-echoes down the narrow street. Luis hears the waterfall tinkling of breaking glass before a second, more powerful blast signals the gas tank of the Lincoln has exploded. The limousine is engulfed in flames. In *El Mercurio* the next morning:

> *MURDER OF SENIOR MILITARY FIGURE:*
> *POLITICAL ASSASSINATION?*
>
> *General Abdón Barrientos, comandante of the Army First Division at Antofagasta and presidential candidate of Partido de Mano Dura, was killed yesterday when a bomb exploded at the intersection of Avenidas Coronel Alvarado and Luis Galdames in the barrio of Independencia. No group has come forward to take credit for this murderous act against the patria, but students of the militant left are being questioned. A small book of poems,* Malas Notas, *was found in the street not far from the crime scene. The author, one Accursio Chiarello, an Argentine poet of questionable talent, has fled the country.*

Meanwhile Accursio, on the lam, slips over the pass into Argentina, taking only enough time to bend his knee in front of the statue of Cristo Redentor at the summit, and then, rising, to extend his long middle finger in the direction of Chile.

Chapter Five

At El Bosco the poets are analyzing the assassination of General Abdón Barrientos. It is clear Accursio has been part of it—since he has hot-footed it back to Argentina, his culpability is undeniable. But why? Has he acted alone? No one suspected Accursio, with his food poetry and his *cocinismo* and his Tamale Sonatas, was political. Had there been hints? The title poem of *Malas Notas*, for example—but hadn't he lauded Barrientos? Or had he panned him? No one could remember; the verse was forgettably mediocre. Whatever Accursio's poetic talent, it did not suggest an accomplished political operative.

How could Accursio have known that Barrientos' limo would be at Alvarado and Goldames at precisely that moment? Only elements in Barrientos' personal bodyguard would have had access to the schedule. An *ultra* right-wing general foregoes appearing on the Santiago grandstand with the *Alcade*, the mayor, in order to play poker in a slummy dive with his girlfriend? Something stinks.

The girlfriend, Piedad? A lefty and a worker? Why would a general of Barrientos' stature take up with her kind? It makes no sense. Something is rotten.

And the strange precursor to the whole . . . the prescient *La Bomba* reading. Was that when Accursio was becoming unhinged? Someone or something must have been using him.

Smoke rings rise above the scarred wooden table. The students Santiago Del Campo and Hector Körner Bulnes have been taken in for questioning. The detectives have hard questions about Santiago's speech at the Club

Unión—he was singling out Barrientos as an impediment? Signaling to someone?

"So they're in jail?" asked Miller Williams.

"Of course not," said Lihn, with his Roman libertine smile. "The godfathers got them out. I doubt they served a minute."

Ever since Valparaiso, Luis had seen Wefe differently. Had she changed? She seemed smaller. Light didn't pool around her anymore. Luis would return from El Bosco or the Café Iris or La Casa de las Botellas and see the light under her door. He'd knock.

She was not too busy, too tired, now. She would be sitting cross-legged on her bed, the abalone shell overflowing with cigarette butts. She would light and squash cigarette after cigarette until her pack of Gauloises was empty. "Luis!" She wanted to talk.

Santiago had given her an unpleasant surprise toward the end of summer. The big party at Pablo Neruda's? His mother had insisted Santiago take his fiancée. Fred Langhorst would have to serve as Wefe's escort. And who was this sudden fiancée?

Odalís Luco Errázuriz.

The mothers were planning the wedding for June. Now it was time for Santiago to assume the duties of a husband-to-be. Of course he and Wefe would remain involved, but they would be more discreet. Many married men had a mistress. Sometimes more than one. Santiago's view was that Wefe had the makings of an excellent mistress. She was very European in her outlook. But Odalís would make a much more reliable wife for a young lawyer like himself with political ambitions.

Luis noticed strange little watercolors, disturbing ones, in dark colors, pinned to the walls. She wanted to talk and talk and talk and talk. The reasons for the break-up. Santiago had so much love to give. No one woman could

90

take all the love he had to give. He had a big heart. Luis doubted it was Santiago's heart that was so big. Was Odalís beautiful? Or only pretty? Luis lied. There were flaws in the beauty. She was fat. She wasn't really intelligent. There was something weird about her mouth. She was nothing more than a pretty little pig who went oink oink oink with her strange mouth. Luis would demonstrate. Wefe would have to laugh. A strained laugh.

Sometimes Luis asked his own questions. Abdón Barrientos. The bomb. What had she known? To which Wefe at first gave oblique, incomplete answers, interrupted by the lighting, then squashing, of a cigarette.

Then she told him. She and Santiago had been out all night. They landed back at Villavicencio early Sunday morning. After sex they started quarreling about Odalís. All during their argument, there had been voices in the living room. It seemed Hector had some people over. They were too busy fighting to pay much attention to Hector. She had been in tears, hysterical. She hadn't wanted to leave, but she also hadn't wanted to stay.

She had stumbled into the living room. There was Hector in the act of unpinning a huge Chilean flag. Under it, a map of Santiago with a smeared red X. Hector had raced to an easel and flipped over sheets of paper as fast as he could, but not before she had seen a diagram of a bomb. After that she started to wonder what was going on. Her suspicions had been raised. Why was Hector Körner Bulnes on the phone all the time talking baby talk? Hector and Accursio huddled together, their black pea-jackets pulled up to their ears, in various cafes on the Alemeda? Those two had never been friends before. Something was up.

So should she have said something to Luis at that time? Yes, but he was never around, he was spending all his time with that Stella Diaz Varín; and she and Santiago were drinking too much and smoking too much, and

Santiago had just thrust upon her the news of Odalís, so she was all tearful and snotty-nosed and feeling sorry for herself. So she really couldn't think about what the map and the bomb diagram might mean for Luis's book, until the day of Neruda's party. Then, watching Santiago with Odalís, her vision shifted a notch. The veil lifted. She suddenly saw a lot of things.

Then Wefe yanks the conversation back to herself. She says the break-up was actually her decision. "He's really bourgeois. I'm an artist."

"So—come back to Berkeley with me." Luis asks out of loyalty.

Wefe strikes her weary, woman-of-the-world pose. He hasn't seen this pose for some time. "I'm an artist. I don't have to have a man in my life every minute. *I vant to be alone.*" She flashes him a smile, the first time she has smiled for weeks.

She's sticking by her story, and Luis admires that.

They take a long time to say good-bye to each other. He is ready to go. But he will be going back to Berkeley without the girl he came with, who had been part of him, part of his psyche, part of his soul. Now a stern angel of her solitude. He has to respect that.

All of October as it moves into November, feels like the dark woods, *el bosco oscuro,* all over again. He dreams of the well again, and this time it is his own face he sees, fractured, at the bottom of the dark chute. What does that mean? He pulls away from Stella—that live wire, that hot spot. She is too hot for him. She lets him withdraw. He feels the attraction, but he won't act on it ever again. He does not want an affair with an old lady, a woman who will stay with a man like Tito Bustos because of his big *pijo.* It was an underworld out there in Maipu. The shouting. The cheap incense. The cat's piss. It felt low class and violent.

Stella was a pitfall he had narrowly missed. There is one ray of sunlight in the forest. He is a published poet now. A violet-scented card arrives with a Berkeley telephone number and the scrawl, "Call me!" He is a young lion, and the thought is a gleam in the dark woods.

The second week of November Luis took a taxi out to the house on Alvaro Casanova. He had come by himself. He had not wanted to share this last visit to Nicanor with anyone—not Stella, not Armando Menedín, not Miller Williams. He paid the driver and got off at the intersection of Larrain and Alvaro Casanova. It was a quarter mile to Parra's place. He wanted to walk.

It had rained overnight. Rectangles of white light shone in black puddles on the road. Pink oleanders and a tangle of vines cascaded over the stone wall to his left. Beyond a sloping hillside of bleached grass, bare earth and rocks lay all of Santiago de Chile, the city sprawled out in the bowl which was the Santiago Basin. He could make out Cerro San Cristobal, Cerro Santa Lucia—the square towers of the Iglesia de San Agustin and Basilica de La Merced. The lane smelled of eucalyptus and jasmine, sun and dust, fresh horse droppings. A man wearing the flat black hat of a *huaso* passed him on horseback, his torso swaying.

Nicanor was waiting for him under the *maitén* tree. The dark-haired woman placed a bottle of carménère on the table, silently, and two glasses.

Luis drew a copy of *The Calculated Lion* out of his bag. "It's for you." Luis had written in it. For Nicanor Parra. *El maestro.*

"Thank you," said Parra, gravely.

They leaned back in the heat of the afternoon. The carménère was followed by a pitcher of sangría. The little birds sang *Luisito. Poeta. Luisito. Poeta.*

The assassination. Could Accursio have been involved? Parra looked away. The Argentine could have been used. Abdón Barrientos no doubt had enemies, even within the military he thought he controlled. One thing was clear. That FeCH student with the clean-cut good looks had nothing to do with it. Calling him in was only a ploy to put people off the trail. Parra couldn't remember the young man's name.

"Santiago Del Campo?"

"Ah, yes. Del Campo. Not a bad family."

"But how about his roommate—Körner Bulnes?"

"Körner Bulnes? Oh, much more likely. That family is close to Agustín Edwards. But, Luis, it's not wise to look closely at the underside of Chilean politics."

A different question—one Luis had to ask. Stella Diaz Varín. What was Nicanor's assessment? He remembered her discourse on *pijos*. As a poet, he added.

A grin broke out on Parra's face. "Have you read La Vibora?"

> *For many years I was sentenced to worship*
> *   a despicable woman,*
> *To sacrifice myself for her, to suffer untold humiliation*
> *   and ridicule,*
> *To work day and night to feed and clothe her,*
> *to carry out certain crimes, to commit certain offenses*
> *. . .*
> *I lived many years a prisoner of the charm of this*
> *woman*
> *who used to present herself in my office completely*
> *naked,*
> *executing contortions the most difficult to imagine,*
> *with the purpose of incorporating my poor soul*
> *   into her orbit,*
> *and, above all, to extort from me my last cent.*

"So la vibora is Stella?"

Parra's black brows wiggled up and down. *"Te gusta?"*

"Sí."

"El poema, o la mujer?" asked Nicanor, wickedly.

"Los dos," replied Luis, diplomatically. "So la vibora *is* Stella."

"La vibora es todos mujeres—o ningunas. Remember, *sea amigo con la ambigüedad."* The older poet had an enormous grin.

And that was all Luis could get out of him on the topic of Stella.

They parted after a few hours. Nicanor reminded Luis to look up his good friend, Fernando Alegría, who would be teaching at Berkeley in the spring.

October passed into November. It was spring in Chile. Acacias had been flowering for weeks, and blue latifolias and orange alonsoas, pink oleanders, the white trumpet flower called *florabundo*. From California came another reminder that the Mertins Fellowship ended December 31, 1963. It was time to go home.

Luis and Stella were drinking pisco sours at a new dive they liked called the Casa Verde. At the bar two old waiters in white aprons talked to one another. A fixture above the bar cast a harsh light. The face of a customer on a barstool was shadowed; the light reflected on his eyeglasses. A small radio over the bar blared American swing music.

A group entered, scraping their chairs against the floor as they sat down. They exuded bonhomie, leaning into one another, embracing with arms outstretched like octopuses, their open mouths showing their upper teeth. One female was convulsed with laughter on her friend's shoulder. A genial group. The old servers straightened as the group took its place, but they did not move away from the bar. An announcement interrupted the scratchy music. Walter Cronkite, reporting from CBS news:

> *In Dallas, Texas, three shots were fired at President Kennedy's motorcade in downtown Dallas. First reports say that President Kennedy has been seriously wounded by this shooting.*

Minutes later,

> *There has been an attempt on the life of President Kennedy. He was wounded in an automobile driving from Dallas Airport into downtown Dallas, along with Governor Connelly of Texas. They have been taken to Parkland Hospital where their condition is as yet unknown.*

Presidents don't get shot in the United States. That only happened in poor undemocratic countries. Oh, sure, people *do* get shot in the United States—in the arm, through the shoulder. Hunting accidents. They survive. Kennedy would survive. Surely. The blows kept coming in waves.

> *NBC is reporting that President Kennedy is dead. Father Huber has administered the last rites.*

> *A news bulletin from Walter Cronkite. From Dallas, Texas, the flash, apparently official. President Kennedy died at one pm Central Standard time. Some thirty-eight minutes ago.*

*Vice-President Lyndon B. Johnson is
taking the oath of office aboard Air Force
One on its way back to Washington, DC.*

This did not happen in America. Was it a coup? Something from Russia? Was an atomic attack next? He had to find Wefe, find Fred. He had to be with his own people. Stella was staring at him. He gave her a kiss on the cheek. "I'm heading home."

"Be careful, Luisito," she said.

Be careful of what? It was something to say. No one knew what was happening. In a trance he walked Huérfanos, Miraflores, Merced, past Plaza Baquedano, down Providencia to Condell and the Casa de los Falcones.

Wefe and Fred sat in the living room watching television. CBS and NBC played the same footage over and over. The motorcade. Jackie in her pillbox hat. The President, waving. The scene at Parkland Memorial Hospital. Kennedy's personal physician stating the President was dead. Luis sat down with them. Wefe made cocoa. The three spent the rest of the evening watching the television. What did this mean for America?

Luis's farewell book party was subdued. Armando Menedín gave a little speech. He acknowledged Luis as a rising star and thanked Miller Williams for writing the introduction. But the Kennedy buzz was non-stop.

"How did they find the guy so fast?" "Then Ruby shoots him two days later?" "Convenient to kill him before he proves his innocence." "An assassination in Texas, and a Texan becomes President?" The naiveté of Americans amazed Chileans. Could this have anything to do with Abdón Barrientos? Had Barrientos known something he shouldn't have? Was it payback from Castro for the numerous CIA assassination plots against him?"

The party is dissipating when Wefe arrives by herself. Luis, Stella, and Wefe sit at a wood table scarred with initials, hearts, indecipherable hieroglyphs, drunken inspirations of the past. From whiskeys and pisco sours, they have moved on *aguardiente*. The evening gets sloshy. Wefe looks like she is going to cry. "Weepy Wefe," says Luis, clumsily patting her arm.

"Loopy Luis," burbles Wefe. She gives them both a drunken smile.

Stella unlooses her usual string of obscentities. "The world is filled with *coños*." She hiccups. "Everyone pretending to be something they're not. Your *novio*, my husband—*maricones* pretending they're *macho* men."

Wefe burps.

"*Qué es la vida?*," intones Luis. He puts his arms around both his women. It is all coming back to him. Lope de Vega. Or is it Calderón? "*Qué es la vida? Una ilusión. Una sombra. Una ficción.*"

The Mertins Foundation would be proud of him.

Luis is flying home, one hundred copies of *The Calculated Lion* packed in his big suitcase, the pages smelling of ink. In Berkeley sunset will come early and it will rain, but here at Panahuel airport the temperature is eighty degrees and the air has a pinkish glow. The plane lifts, circles, and then points north, toward Peru, Ecuador. California. He watches out the window for a last view of the Andes.

The jagged angles of the cordillera are blue-black against the sky. They are a series of expressionless shaman faces. And the mountain nearest him lowers its eyelid for a second in one long, knowing wink.

Epilogue

In 1970 Allende becomes President of Chile and nationalizes the copper industry. On September 11, 1973, General Agustín Pinochet bombs the presidential palace. Allende does not survive. Then follow eighteen years of military dictatorship, fully but covertly supported by US industrial interests and the CIA.

Wefe Langhorst returns to Europe where she exhibits her watercolors and other art and dies at age sixty of lung cancer. Santiago Del Campo has a distinguished career as a diplomat and public servant, thanks to his *vía de la mitad* in which he always finds himself at the fulcrum of the political equation. Of Osvaldo Güareí nothing is known. Stella Diaz Varín is honored in 1994 by Cuba's Casa de las Americas for a lifetime of leftist poetry and dies in 2006 of throat cancer, her actual age still a matter of dispute. Nicanor Parra lives in Las Cruces, Chile, and is frequently mentioned for a Nobel in literature.

Luis Garcia lives in Berkeley, a much-loved figure on the poetry scene. He has published fifteen books of poetry including *A Message from Garcismo*, *A Wheel in the Sky*, and *The Sleeping Gypsy*. Luis will give one of his incomparable jazzed-up poetry readings at the Mythos Gallery on March 29, 2014.

And what of Accursio Chiarello, Hector Körner Bulnes, Ramón Gúareí and Jesús? Accursio, despairing of making money from poetry, becomes a chef in Recoleta; his delicatessen (which he names Menu de Cualquier) is famous for its alfajores. Ramón Gúareí works as a labor organizer and is rounded up in 1973 with the folksinger Victor Jara and thousands of others and shot to death in Santiago's Municipal Stadium. Jesús, with his Christ-like demeanor, proves one of the most fanatical and focused of the revolutionary students. He ambushes Hector Körner Bulnes one dark night at the intersection of Estado and Huérfanos, leaving him to die on the very spot where, years before, a vagabond saxophonist played What Is This Thing Called Love.

The shamans of the Andes keep their eyes open and their mouths shut, according to their own timetable, signifying their displeasure with occasional murderous or violent rumblings. Then on February 27, 2010, having seen enough, they erupt in maniacal laughter, felt in Chile as its 8.9 Bio-Bio earthquake, the second largest ever recorded on our planet.

Gail Chiarello
Seattle, Washington
January 10, 2014